Flora Flowerdew & the Mystery of the Duke's Diamonds

FLORA FLOWERDEW VICTORIAN MYSTERIES, BOOK 1

AMANDA MCCABE

PUBLISHER'S NOTE: This is a work of fiction. Names, characters, places, and incidents either are the product of the author's imagination or are used fictitiously. Any resemblance to actual persons, living or dead, business establishments, events, or locales is entirely coincidental.

Flora Flowerdew and the Mystery of the Duke's Diamonds 2022
Copyright © Amanda McCabe

Published by Oliver-Heber Books

0 9 8 7 6 5 4 3 2 1

One

LONDON, 1888

"Will you all join hands, please?" Madame Flora Flowerdew said in her soft, serious, mysterious 'spirit medium' voice. She tried not to sigh with boredom as she gave a serene smile to the people gathered around her table. This was the fourth séance in a week, and while she was certainly grateful for the bread and butter the 'seekers' provided, she would give anything for something *different* to happen.

She glanced at her Pomeranian dog, Chou-Chou, who sat contentedly on her cushion in the corner, cleaning her paw. She was calm and quiet, which meant Flora could expect no spiritual assistance that night. It was all on her.

Flora bit back another sigh. She couldn't remember now why she had thought setting up as a medium would be preferable to the stage at the Follies. It was really just the same. Put on the costume, paint on a face, prance out in front of the audience, and sparkle, sparkle, sparkle. Everything was just one big performance.

She had to admit the salary for seances was a tiny bit better than the stage. She could pay for her nice Kensington flat—at the *respectable* end of the district. And it

1

kept Chou-Chou in ground chicken and herself in pretty clothes. But lud, it was weary-making sometimes.

She studied the four people gathered around her table on that night. They were the usual sort of customers for that sort of thing. People who claimed to have important questions for the beyond, and the pounds and pence to pay for it. A baronet and his wife, and their pretty daughter, who was said to be almost engaged to a duke. Sir Henry had also brought his maiden sister to make up the numbers, but Miss Priscilla Petrie looked as bored as Flora felt.

She'd been able to find out little enough about their errand, despite her usual leading questions. She always 'interviewed' the customers before a session, to decide if she would take them on. It gave her business an air of exclusivity which people liked, and gave her a chance to see how easy the case might be. If it was a one-time thing, like someone trying to find Granny's pearl ring, or if they were looking to be a regular. Regulars brought in a nice income stream, but they were more exhausting than the one-and-dones. They were usually looking for a hand to hold, someone they could bare their soul to in discretion, and Flora was good at that.

She didn't really know what Sir Henry and his family needed, except for wanting 'Maudie,' the pretty daughter, to be sure of her future security. Flora assumed that meant the almost-fiancé duke, but surely a private detective would be more help than a medium. But she did feel rather sorry for Maudie, who looked strangely sad for a future duchess, and agreed to take the Petries on. Maybe she could at least reassure the girl that a future of strawberry leaves wasn't so bad. As if anyone should need reassurance about *that*.

Flora gestured to Mary, her maid and sometimes-assistant, to lower the lamps as everyone around the table clasped hands. Just as the room faded to one small, flickering point of light in the middle of the table, Flora caught a glimpse of herself in the silver-framed mirror on the opposite wall. For just a second, she was a bit startled at the stranger she saw there, which was silly. She had pretended to be someone else every day of her adult life, both on the stage and off. Yet something about that coal-black wig in its elaborate curls and braids, that stark-white powdered face above a high, jet-beaded collar, always surprised her.

Then she remembered. She wasn't Florrie Grubbins, chorus girl, any more. She was Madame Flora Flowerdew, medium extraordinaire. She had to look the part. No one would trust their ghostly needs to a young (well, young*ish*) strawberry blonde from Poplar in the East End.

Sir Henry took his wife's hand firmly, while poor Lady Petrie looked so scared she trembled. Flora wished she could tell her nothing scary was going to happen, maybe just a bit of table-shaking if the mood was right. But that would ruin the whole project. Miss Petrie looked faintly interested now, and Maudie still just looked sad and distant. She took her aunt's hand and stared off into the shadows with her pretty, pale distraction. Flora thought she wouldn't make a half-bad medium herself, if duchessing didn't work out.

As the lights dimmed, Flora placed her fingertips on the crystal ball in front of her and closed her eyes. The small room was always kept very warm, the windows muffled in dark red velvet draperies, old-fashioned tapestries of mysterious ancient Greek rituals on the walls. The only furniture was the round mahogany table and straight-backed chairs, and one console where Mary tended the objects that might be needed in the course of an evening, like the planchet board and bottles of sherry if anyone fainted.

Flora had to admit she rather liked the beginning of a séance. The warmth and darkness, the moments when she closed her eyes and could hear only the breathing of

3

the people around her, were all quite relaxing. She didn't know how to go into a real trance, of course, but it was a little like a moment out of time. All the rehearsal was done, and there was only the performance before her.

She concentrated on the Petries. She might not be able to read minds, but her time on the stage gave her a certain insight into characters. She hoped she could read them right that evening, find out what they wanted.

She took a deep breath, and summoned up her medium voice, a tone much deeper and rougher than her own carefully modulated accent. "We call upon the spirit world. We have need of you."

She sensed Maud stiffen next to her, as if the girl had been startled out of her sad distraction. "Can you help me?" she gasped.

"Maud," her father growled. "You can't interfere."

"But I need to know!" Maud insisted.

Flora concentrated on her, on that burst of desperation. Maud's energy suddenly seemed like a living thing, and Flora wondered if being a duchess was always such a good thing after all, if it caused so much distress. Or maybe Maud was afraid the strawberry leaves would suddenly be snatched away?

She almost reached for the girl's hand, but something most alarming happened. She was pinned to her chair by an unseen force, cold and slippery but inescapable. She couldn't breathe, and the darkness whirled around her. She tried to grasp the crystal ball, to throw it at whatever had invaded her room, but she was trapped. A bitter rush of panic clawed its way up her throat.

"What is happening?" Lady Petrie screamed.

Flora didn't know. Nothing like that had ever happened to her before. Even when Chou-Chou found a real spirit in the ether, which wasn't often but did sometimes happen, it didn't go like this at all. A cold wind raced around the room, whipping at the tapestries,

4

making Lady Petrie scream even louder. Flora wished she could scream herself, but her throat was frozen.

"My goodness!" Miss Petrie said, sounding quite excited. "This *is* interesting."

Chou-Chou barked and growled, and Flora heard it all as if from a great distance. It was like watching events in a play, but also being plopped into the very middle of the mayhem and doom of the plot with no script as guidance. Fascinating—and terrifying.

A smell rose up around them, like expensive soap, the country earth after a rain, and brandy. Very strong brandy. *At least it's not rotting flesh*, Flora thought, desperate to feel reassured that they weren't being invaded by demons or elementals or something else horrid.

"There can't be a duchess without the diamonds!" a man shouted. It was a rough, irascible voice, filled with raw fury. The glass windows behind the drapes rattled.

"What do you mean?" Flora managed to squeak.

"The diamonds are gone. There can be no duchess until they're returned," he shouted again, and he sounded a bit cross that she hadn't gathered that already. "Find the diamonds, or it is the end of the Evertons. It's the curse. Isn't that why you called me?"

"I—don't know," Flora whispered. "Who *are* you?"

"The Duke of Everton!" he roared, and it was like a train blasting along the tracks, blowing everything out of its path.

"That's nonsense," Sir Henry spluttered. "The duke is engaged to *my* daughter. The Evertons will continue."

"Not without the diamonds!" the spirit insisted. "Find them, and the family will be well. Tell my useless grandson. He must know to cease being foolish. His father..."

The roar was fading, the room growing warmer again, as if his force was retreating. Flora found she could suddenly move again, and she grabbed the crystal ball, clutching at its familiar weight. It felt hot against

5

her palm. Sir Henry shot up from his chair and pushed the table, almost overturning it. Lady Petrie shrieked.

"Tell him! The diamonds must be found," the spirit shouted one more time. For just a fleeting instant, Flora glimpsed a white face in the shadows. Old, heavy-jowled, wreathed with a gray mustache, he looked terribly fierce. Then the vision vanished, and the room went perfectly still.

"I told you," Maud whispered, her voice choked with tears. "I can't marry him!"

"Don't be a fool," her father snapped. "My grandfather worked in a coal mine. You can be a duchess. That's the way it's going to be, and no flimflammery can stop it."

"What *did* happen here?" Miss Priscilla Petrie gasped.

Flora gestured to Mary to turn up the lamps again. The light illuminated the shambles of the séance, the table pushed askew, the curtains crooked at the windows. Lady Petrie sobbed into her handkerchief.

"This isn't what I paid for," Sir Henry said, his craggy face bright red.

"Sometimes the spirits will not be controlled," Flora said, her head heavy with weariness. She had said such things before, of course, when she sensed a customer wanted a lively séance to tell their friends about. She had never really seen it before. Lud, she had never even seen a *ghost* before. It was usually Chou-Chou who had powers.

She frowned as she looked at the spot where the face had been, uncertain what had actually happened.

"I told you, I can't marry him," Maud insisted. "Especially not with—with *that* following me about."

"Surely it can't be too hard to find these diamonds," Flora said, more intrigued than ever by the Petries' story and how they had become involved with these jewel-misplacing Evertons. "That does seem to be all he wants,

and then I am sure he will return to his rightful plane."
She studied the jostled table. "Of course, we may have to
hold another séance. The circle was broken before it
could be properly closed. I am sure the spirit would tell
us more then."

Flora swallowed hard. She really didn't want to meet
the angry late duke again, but business was business.

"This was no help at all," Sir Henry raged. He took
his sobbing wife's arm and pulled her up from her chair.
"We are going now."

He rushed his wife and sister out of the room, Mary
scrambling to keep up and fetch their wraps. Maud
grasped Flora's fingers and whispered frantically, "You
must help me, Madame Flowerdew! I really can't marry
him, diamonds or not."

"Maudie!" her father shouted.

Flora felt quite sorry for the girl, who did look so
pale and desperate. "I will try," she said.

Maud looked a bit relieved. She nodded and rushed
out after her parents.

Flora slowly rose from her chair, her legs shaking so
much she was sure she would fall right down. She heard
Chou-Chou whimper, and she turned to scoop the little
dog up into her arms. Chou-Chou licked her chin, and
Flora buried her face in the warm, caramel-colored fluff
of the dog's cottony fur.

"That was most—unusual, wasn't it, sweetie-
lumkins?" she whispered, and Chou-Chou blinked her
amber eyes.

Unusual, to say the least. She wondered about the
old duke's diamonds and what might have happened to
them. She didn't know much about the ducal family at
all, except that the new duke had only held his title for
less than a year, and Maud Petrie was going to (maybe)
marry him.

Mary came back after the Petries were gone, and she
plopped down in a chair, her black poplin parlor-maid

dress rumpled around her and her ruffled white cap askew.

"Well," she said, her Bow Bells accent coming out again. "That was a helluva ride, wasn't it?"

"To say the least," Flora muttered. "I think this calls for a bottle of port, don't you, Mary? The good stuff."

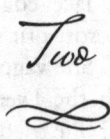

Two

Flora woke up late the next morning, feeling rather out of sorts after the strange doings of the night before and the rich port. She always had a slight headache following some seances, nothing a strong cup of tea and a bit of fresh air couldn't fix.

Yet that day felt different. Her whole body ached, as it hadn't since her time of doing high kicks and spins every night at the Follies, and the single ray of grayish sunlight peeking through the bedroom curtains set her head pounding. Flora groaned and rolled over on her pillows, wishing she'd had a few more hours of sleep. Or maybe days of it.

For an instant, she was startled by a head floating in her dressing table mirror. She shot up with a yelp, only to fall back again. It was just her black "madame" wig on its stand.

"Silly goose," she said, and tugged the blankets around her again. Chou-Chou snuffled in objection at being tossed from her little nest of cushions, but soon settled down again, falling into snoring doggie sleep.

Flora wished she could do the same. Tired as she had been after the Petries stormed away, she had stayed up far too long trying to decipher what had happened. Had

9

a real ghost truly shown up? Why did he choose her house, out of all the spirit mediums in London? What did he want?

She picked at the lace edge of her coverlet and frowned as she tried to sort out something that seemed to make no sense at all. She vaguely remembered something more to do with the Evertons, something scandalous, but what was it? She tried to keep up with all the Society gossip. Knowing people was her stock in trade, after all. It seemed as if whatever had happened was quite some time ago, though, and she realized she didn't know much at all about the new duke. Only that he might or might not marry Miss Petrie. If the diamonds were found.

Lost diamonds. It all sounded very intriguing. Like a story in one of the penny dreadfuls Flora guiltily consumed.

There was a quick knock at the door, and Mary bustled in efficiently with the morning tray of tea and toast. The gray skirts of her day dress rustled as she sat the tray down and tugged open the curtains, letting in the full light of day. Or as much light as there was to be had in London, anyway.

"Good morning, Miss Flora! How'd you sleep, then?" Mary said, far too cheerful. She was one of those creatures Flora loathed the most—a morning person. But Flora had to admit she had become a spectacular maid. Mary had started life on the East End streets, and like Flora herself had to reinvent herself, beginning as a dresser at the Follies. Their start in Kensington had been a bit rocky, but Flora thought they were making do quite nicely now.

"Not very well," Flora grumped. She buttered her toast as she watched Mary pick up the "madame" gown where it was left draped over the chaise last night. Mary studied the dark purple satin, and tsked at a couple of loose jet beads. Madame dresses did not come cheap. "What do you make of what happened last night?"

"Spooky," Mary said with a shudder. "Whoever that was, he wasn't fooling around."

"So it wasn't you?" Flora had half-hoped it *was* Mary, who sometimes helped a slow session along with the assistance of some pulleys and shuttered lamps. Yet Flora always knew about that ahead of time and could work with it.

Mary firmly shook her head. The streamers of her cap fluttered against her brown curls. "Not me, miss. I don't mind admitting I hid under the hall table when I heard all that racket. I thought maybe it was *you*."

"No. A real ghost, then? That's strange." The toast suddenly tasted as dry as ashes in her mouth. She took a quick gulp of tea.

"He's not going to just go away, is he?" Mary said.

"We can hope so, but I doubt it. He sounded very determined."

"A right gasper, if you ask me."

"What do you know about the Evertons?"

Mary frowned in thought as she swiped a dust cloth over the scent bottles and powder pots on the dressing table. "Not much. They have that big house over on Green Park, I think, used to have lots of parties there. Before my time."

"Maybe the diamonds were stolen at one of those parties?"

Mary pursed her lips. "My old friend Pete, that was his territory once. But he'd never carry off anything like that. Just a bit of pickpocketing and the like. It would take a real professional to steal some duke's diamonds. No one I ever knew was on that level. I can try to find Pete, though, see if he knows of anything."

"That would be very helpful, Mary. I think I'll head over to the *Evening Star*, see if Evelyn remembers any Everton story."

"That writer friend of yours?"

"The very one." Flora had met Evelyn Finnegan when Evie used to write a column of theater reviews and gossip. Evie had since gone on to more important articles about Parliament and crime (sometimes one in the same), and Flora kept in touch with her. She always had the most fascinating nuggets of news about the city's more colorful citizens, both high and low. "She's sure to know something. I do have the feeling we haven't quite heard the last of the late duke."

~

An hour later, Flora set off from her flat to catch the omnibus to Evie's office in Fleet Street. She had left her heavy, dark medium's garb behind, wearing her own amethyst and cream striped walking dress and purple kid boots. Mary had expertly curled and pinned her strawberry-blonde hair and set a jaunty, feathered tricorn hat on top.

Flora always felt better as herself, if not as confident as she was in the Madame Flowerdew disguise, and hummed a tune as she hurried along, pulling on her gloves. The answers were surely out there, just waiting to be found!

The day had become an unusually sunny one for London, the pea-souper that had plagued them the week before lifting to reveal a patch of actual blue sky. Well, more a grayish sky, to be sure, Flora thought as she peered up toward the clouds, but a real sky nevertheless. It seemed like everyone else wanted to revel in it, too, for the sidewalks were crowded around her. Businessmen in their dark suits and bowler hats, rolled newspapers under their arms, jostled for spare space with well-upholstered matrons in fur-trimmed tippets and velvet toques, nursery maids shepherding their pinafored charges, and liveried footmen on errands.

Flora paused to study a dressmaker's window, decorated with rolls of bright silks, spools of ribbons, red cashmere shawls, and a basket overflowing with fluffy ostrich plumes needed for Court presentations. Next door was a bookseller and stationer, their display a gleaming pyramid of leather-bound volumes in green and garnet-red and chocolate-brown, stamped in gold. They didn't put the penny dreadfuls Flora herself bought from them in the front.

She was still amazed that *this* was where she lived now. A place with clean streets and pretty shop windows, prosperous passers-by and carriages rumbling past drawn by glossy-maned horses. It was so different from where she grew up, the mucky lanes and stench of rotting produce and tanneries everywhere. Crowds and noise and fights breaking out with no warning. She couldn't believe that reflection in the glass, of a lady with a fashionable gown and curled hair, was really her.

She heard the clatter of the omnibus stopping at the corner, and she jumped over a mud puddle to climb aboard, digging her coin out of her reticule. It wasn't very crowded at that time of day, mostly ladies on shopping errands and gentlemen on their way from their offices to lunch, and she quickly found a seat where she could watch the streets slide past and think about what happened last night.

She got off at the end of Evie's lane. It was very different from the wide walkways and green parks of her own neighborhood, all tall, narrow, soot-streaked brick buildings, a few coffee houses and pubs. Everyone there seemed in a great hurry, every space humming with commerce and busy bustle.

Inside the *Evening Star* office it was even louder. The clatter of printers and click of typewriters was almost drowned out by shouted questions and curses. It was like music, Flora thought as she dodged around newsboys and ink-stained typesetters to make her way up the narrow stairs. The warm air smelled thick with ink, paper, and dust. It was strange, modern music, to be sure, all noise and speed and steam. It was very exciting, but all in all she preferred her new work in her own cozy flat.

Evie's office was at the end of the upstairs corridor, a bit quieter than the main floor but almost as chaotic. Secretaries and editors hurried past on errands, their arms filled with file folders. Flora knocked quickly at the door before she pushed it open. Evie sat behind her desk, her booted feet propped on its edge, the hem of her tweed split skirt falling back to show her muddy stacked heels. The light from the windows turned her unruly bright red curls to fire.

She was using her lorgnette to study a sheet of sketches, and she barely glanced up at Flora's sudden entrance. "Oh, it's you, Florrie," she said. "Come take a look at this. It's fascinating."

Curious, Flora peeked over Evie's shoulder, only to draw back at the sight of a woman being stabbed, her mouth open in a scream. "Revolting."

"Isn't it just? That hideous murder in Whitechapel. Our lead story in tomorrow's edition." She put down the paper and watched as Flora dropped into the chair across from the desk. "But I guess you aren't here about prostitutes being murdered."

"Not today, no." Flora drew off her gloves with a sigh. "I wanted to see if you knew anything about the Duke of Everton."

"Everton?" Evie tapped her knuckles thoughtfully on the edge of her desk. "Of Thornhill Abbey? I think maybe he was godfather to one of the queen's brats."

"Well, considering those brats are all grown and married now, that must have been in his more active days. I think he's dead now, because he burst into my séance last night. Uninvited."

Evie's eyes widened. "Really? Oh, do tell!"

Evie was always fascinated by Flora's work, hoping it would give her a nugget of news anyone undead couldn't know. So far there'd been nothing, but Flora had a feeling that was about to change. She quickly told Evie about the Petries and their odd evening.

"Diamonds, you say?" Evie said. She hurried to the row of filing cabinets along the back wall of her office and started digging through the dusty folders. "I think there *was* something, but I can't remember the details. It was long before my time here, or even back when I was on the theater review pages."

"Back when we were all young and full of spring-time hope," Flora said with a laugh. "When I could kick ever so high, and wasn't reduced to spending my evenings summoning up Grandmama to find out where she hid her garnet brooch."

"Well, I think this goes beyond Granny's garnets," Evie said, triumphantly pulling an old photograph from her files. "Behold the Duchess of Everton in her famous diamonds!"

"Really? Let me see!" Flora reached for the image and studied it in excitement. It was rather faded, a portrait of a very stately lady, tall and full-bosomed in the crinoline fashions of twenty years ago. Her dark hair was swept high, and crowned with a diamond tiara that was so large it resembled nothing so much as a fence. A tall, spiky tipped fence made of sparkle. Around her neck was a matching necklace, with a double-tiered brooch on her dark, low-cut bodice and bracelets on each gloved wrist.

"The Everton diamonds," she sighed. If the duke had indeed lost them, she could see why he would come back from the dead to retrieve them. They were stunning, better than anything the queen herself owned.

"It says here that Her Grace is now living in retirement in the South of France, but her husband just shuffled off the mortal coil last year," Evie said, reading a clipping in the same file. "Their grandson is now the duke, since their only son died ages ago. He was a famous explorer, always off to the Amazon or Africa."

"So the grandson must be Miss Petrie's betrothed," Flora said. "Is there anything in there that talks about the diamonds being lost?"

Evie shook her head. "But there are a few more files upstairs. I can take a look there later today."

Flora studied the sparkle of the diamonds, star-bright even in the faded photo. "That would be smashing, Evie. I'd love to find out what old dukie is so upset about."

"Are you going to summon him up again? Can I be there when you do?"

"I don't really know what I'm going to do. I told the Petries the circle needs to be properly closed, but they didn't seem in a hurry to give it a try." She knew what she probably *should* do. Send Sir Henry a bill, and then forget all about them and the Evertons. They were trouble she didn't need. But when had that ever stopped her before? And she had to admit she *was* very curious. What had really happened at her séance table last night? Where were the diamonds?

She thanked Evie, promised to invite her to the next séance, and left the office to go home and tend to her own tasks. She had another séance scheduled that evening with a regular client who liked to contact his late business partner for investment tips, and she couldn't be late. But all the way back to her flat, she couldn't stop thinking about those blasted diamonds, and the late duke's angry demands. She was so caught up in her thoughts, she almost didn't see the silk hat and man's leather gloves on her foyer table.

"Oh, Madame Flowerdew, thank the skies you're back!" Mary whispered frantically as she hurried out of the sitting room. She only called Flora 'Madame Flowerdew' when clients were there. Chou-Chou peeked out from behind Mary's gray skirts with her wide, caramel doggie eyes. "You have a caller, and he's very insistent on seeing you."

Flora frowned. "Is it Mr. Peabody again? I've told him before, he needs an appointment and..."

"No, not him! It's the Duke of Everton himself."

Three

F
eeling uncharacteristically flustered, Flora left
her hat and gloves with Mary and quickly tidied
her hair as she hurried toward the sitting room.
There was no time to put on her 'madame' guise. There
was a real duke, in her own home. She had a baronet or
two among her clients, and plenty of wealthy mill
owners and merchants, but nothing like a duke. She had
barely even met one before! She hardly knew how a girl
from the East End and the stage ought to talk to one.

Yet she was also very curious. What could he tell her
about his ghostly grandfather and the missing diamonds? Why had he come to her flat at all?

She pushed open the door and stepped inside, her
stomach fluttering a bit. The butterflies turned to agi-
tated finches when she saw the man who stood there.

The duke was very tall and very broad-shouldered,
seeming to take up the whole small, well-furnished sitting room. His hair was tawny-gold, longer than was
fashionable and waving back from the stark, sharp an-
gles of his clean-shaven face. He was dressed in an im-
peccably tailored charcoal-gray suit, but the Savile Row
clothes seemed uncomfortable on him, incongruous.
Flora thought he probably needed a Viking tunic and
furs to really suit him. He was really quite astonishing.

Luckily he was half-turned away from her, looking out the window, and she had a second to compose herself before he turned to face her. Of course his eyes were the bluest she had ever seen, pale and piercing like ice.

"Your Grace," she said, instinctively making a little curtsy. She immediately cursed herself for it. After all, *he* had come to see *her*, in her own home. She wasn't a supplicant. "I am Madame Flowerdew. How can I help you today?"

Those icy eyes swept her up and down, and she had to resist patting her hair to make sure it really was tidy. "You are the ghost woman, then?" he said, his voice as jagged as granite. It suited him perfectly. Really, Flora thought, if she was casting a stage production of *Jane Eyre*, he would be an ideal Mr. Rochester.

She laughed. "I myself am not a ghost, but I can serve as a conduit if they have something to communicate."

His nostrils flared and his jaw tightened, who told her what he thought about *that*. Flora didn't blame him. She'd been a skeptic herself, once upon a time.

"I understand you met with Miss Maud Petrie and her family last night," he said.

"My, word does travel fast." Flora sat down on her favorite blue brocade armchair, and took her time arranging her skirts around her. She waved him to the settee, but he shook his head and started pacing the length of the pink flowered needlepoint carpet. Flora saw that Mary had done her duty and brought in the tea tray, and she poured herself a cup. "I hope your fiancée has quite recovered. She seemed understandably startled at the séance. So many people are when first faced with the beyond."

"She isn't yet my official fiancée, and she is rather more than startled," he said, wheeling around to glare at her. "Her mother says she can't stop crying, and she has

19

refused to see me. She may *never* be my fiancée if this keeps up."

Flora remembered how Miss Petrie had seized her hand, begging for her help. "I am very sorry to hear that." She took a slow sip of tea. "What can I do to help? I did tell Sir Henry another séance might be necessary to fully close the circle. Perhaps that would help to settle Miss Petrie's mind as well."

"Another séance is the last thing any of us needs! I have come to demand that you tell me what really happened last night. What trickery was used to make the Petries believe that my grandfather is angry with them."

"No trickery at all, I assure you, Your Grace," Flora said. It was the truth for once. She was as confused by what happened as the Petries were. "I didn't even know about your family or their diamonds until last night."

His frown flickered, and he started pacing again. "So there *was* talk of the diamonds."

"Yes. He seemed very concerned about them. Rather violently so, even." She was becoming quite dizzy from watching him stride across the floor and back, over and over. "Won't you sit down, and tell me more about how I can help? I am quite hopeless when I'm in the dark about it all."

He scowled, but he did sit down on the edge of the settee. He absolutely dwarfed her delicate furniture. Flora poured out another cup of tea and passed it to him. He looked down into it as if the brew might hold answers.

"I do have something a bit stronger, if that would suit," she said.

He shook his head, the light from the windows turning his hair to a golden lion's mane. "Tea is adequate."

"Excellent. Then what can you tell me about the diamonds? Your grandfather seemed to think they were cursed, and keeping you from marriage."

20

"They've been in the family for many years," he said, his tone flat as if he was reciting something he'd said over and over. "Legend says they originally came from India, belonging to a maharajah. But there is a curse on the stones, and none who own them will be happy."

Flora had once played the doomed queen on stage, and had always been fascinated by her. Another intriguing layer to the diamond story. "Is that where the curse took hold? With Marie Antoinette?"

He shrugged. "Who knows? Such legends often grow up around large jewels, don't they? I have heard it was from the family who first acquired them from a maharajah, by the name of Stillworth. But they never seemed really cursed for my family. My grandmother wore them with no ill consequences. Until my father."

Flora was utterly fascinated. It was better than a play. "What happened to your father?"

"I was just a child then. My father never got along with my grandfather, and he took to going on long voyages."

"The famous explorer of the Amazon and Africa," Flora murmured, remembering the newspaper clipping.

His pale eyes narrowed. "I thought you knew nothing about my family."

Flora didn't want to admit she had been out snooping that morning. "I read it in a paper," she said airily. "I've often thought I'd like to travel myself, if the opportunity arose."

"I doubt you'd like to travel as he did. Tents in the desert, canoes on jungle rivers, snakes and flies and hostile natives."

"Maybe not," Flora admitted, shuddering to think of the snakes. "The South of France and maybe Venice would be more my thing."

"He went to India, I think, and that was where he became convinced the diamonds really were cursed. That they never should have left their homeland so long ago. When he returned to the Abbey, he told my grandfather they must be sent back. That we were all doomed, just like my mother, if they stayed. My mother had borrowed the tiara once for a costume party, and was ill after that until she died."

"But your grandmother is still alive."

He frowned. "Logic had little sway for my father by then. He was obsessed with sending the diamonds back to India."

"I would imagine your grandfather wasn't thrilled by such an idea."

The duke snorted. "Of course he wasn't. The old man didn't have a romantic bone in his body. Those were the *Everton* diamonds, and that was that. He thought my father was a fool, just like my uncle, who was the heir before I was born. He now works in the City, along with his son. They all disliked each other."

"So what happened? Between your father and grandfather?"

"Well, on your proverbial dark and stormy night, my father vanished. And so did the diamonds."

Flora gasped. "He stole them?"

"So it seems. A few months later, my father's body was found in a cave in Cornwall, probably drowned while he was waiting for passage to France. Or at least the bones were wearing my father's clothes."

"But the diamonds weren't with him?"

The duke shook his head. "Haven't been seen since. I seldom saw my grandfather after that, I was off to Eton and Cambridge and then the grand tour, but when I was at the Abbey he always railed about their loss. About my father's weaknesses and bad blood. I'm sure he was watching for signs of it in me."

"Hmm." Flora finished her tea, thinking of that angry spirit that swept through her parlor last night. "It obviously still rankles with him. He seems to think your family can't be free to move forward, to marry, until the diamonds are returned."

"Surely he can see where they are from his perch in the afterlife? If indeed it *was* him who appeared to the Petries."

Flora ignored the dubious little dig. "It doesn't really work that way. The deceased aren't playing a big house party game of hide and seek. But they are often upset about unfinished business. Once that's taken care of, they are able to be at peace."

"I can't imagine my grandfather ever being at peace. He wouldn't ever want to leave the Abbey in anyone else's hands."

"He won't have much choice. He is dead, after all. If the diamonds were found, perhaps he could be brought to see reason." She put her cup down on the tray with a decisive click. "You really have no idea where the diamonds could be?"

"Of course I don't," he growled impatiently. "I was just a child when my father took them. I'm sure someone stole them in Cornwall and they've long been broken up and sold."

That was indeed the most likely scenario, Flora thought, and if that was the case, the curse was unlikely to be broken and the old duke would forever be unappeased. But Flora had never been one to give up easily.

"Very possibly," she said. "But could there be anyone who took them *before* your father died? You said your uncle was done out his heirdom by your father and you. And your grandmother did wear the jewels a lot, didn't she? Does she have a large dower now, or could she have squirreled them away? What about servants? Are there any left who remember that time?"

He frowned again, but this time it looked thoughtful, interested. "They've retired, but there are a few maids and our old butler. He worked for my grandfather for ages.

And there's my nanny, though she's quite dotty now, I fear. My uncle hardly ever talks to us, perhaps he was unhappy to lose the title. And my grandmother doesn't have a large income at all, that's why she moved to France to economize. Not that she seems to economize much. Do you really think any of them might know something?"

"Possibly. Servants do see so much about their employers. It could be worth talking to them. Also, Cornwall is full of smugglers, isn't it? I'm sure one of them would remember such a vast haul as a diamond parure. It seems like the stuff of smuggling legend, doesn't it?" Flora was starting to get a bit excited about the whole thing. It was just like one of her favorite penny dreadfuls!

"How could anyone even get started tracing such a thing? It was so long ago."

He was right. It seemed like the coldest of trails. "I don't know, really. But I think I know where we could start."

"How?"

"With another séance, of course."

Four

Through the fuzzy-tulle shards of sleepy dreams, Flora vaguely heard Mary bustle into the bedchamber and throw open the curtains. There was the clatter of china as she plunked down the breakfast tray.

"Come on now, Miss Flora, time to rise!" Mary said, much too cheerful for Flora's liking. A few snatched hours of sleep and strange dreams of chasing running diamonds did not make a merry-sunshine morning. Not that a morning was ever wonderful. Flora had been of the opinion, ever since her Follies days, that no one should wake up before noon.

She groaned and rolled over, making Chou-Chou growl in protest and burrow deeper under the coverlets. "It can't be time to wake up already. You are just trying to torture me, Mary."

Undeterred, Mary tied back the last of the curtains and let in the full force of the watery London light. "It's past time, gone nine. Mrs. Gibbs comes today, and you know she doesn't like her routine changed. She'll want to get in here as soon as she's done the drawing room."

Of course. Mrs. Gibbs. The woman was rather grim, but she did an excellent job twice a week on the heavy cleaning, which meant Flora never had to redden her own hands again, as she had every day in her better-for-gotten youth. Mrs. Gibbs could never be annoyed—and Flora had to keep making the coin to pay her, which meant finding the duke's diamonds before the whole thing damaged her reputation.

She groaned again and pushed herself up against the pillows, squinting into the light. Mary pressed a cup of tea— extra strong because Mary always knew what was needed— into Flora's hands and buttered some of the toast.

"I did have the strangest dreams, Mary," Flora said, and took a deep gulp of the tea.

"No wonder, miss, with all the to-doings here lately," Mary tsked. "Have you figured out what happened yet?"

Flora sighed. "Not at all. I'm no closer to seeing things clearly than when my séance room got blown over."

"Could it *really* have been a ghost, then?"

"I shouldn't think so," Flora said doubtfully. Chou-Chou blinked her eyes balefully from under the bed-clothes, as if to say she knew differently. And Chou-Chou was the real expert on ghosts. "But then, I doubt it was the Petries playing silly tricks. They didn't seem clever enough, and what would be the purpose? Sir Henry seems to want that coronet for his daughter. Yet what did Maud herself want? She didn't seem all that happy about becoming Her Grace." Flora didn't really understand the girl's attitude, though. The duke had such glorious sea-blue eyes, such broad Viking shoulders, even if he did seem a bit stick-in-the-muddish. Maybe it came of having such a mad father.

Flora glanced at the pile of newspaper articles Evie had sent over about the new duke's explorer father. He really had gotten himself into some scrapes before his strange demise, trekking through jungles, falling into crocodile-infested waters, catching frostbite on distant mountains, climbing pyramids. No wonder the son seemed intent on making the Everton title proper again.

Mary gathered up Flora's clothes from the chair where they were scattered and headed for the door. "I've got to send these off to the laundry before Mrs. Gibbs gets here. You ring when you're ready to dress, Miss Flora, just don't take too long about it, mind. Oh, and the morning post is on the tray. One of those letters looks ever so important."

Flora sorted through the stack of papers, mostly bills alas, and a few notes setting séance appointments. The one on the bottom did look "important" indeed, sealed with a ducal crest. She tore it open and saw it was from the duke of the handsome eyes.

Can we meet again soon? I think I have some ideas about the diamonds. Send word to me about any convenient times at Everton House, Green Park. It was signed "Benedict Everton," terribly informal.

Benedict. So that was his name. Flora sat back against the pillows and fanned herself with the note. She found it smelled faintly of expensive sandalwood. Chou-Chou crawled from her nest and sat up to stare at Flora.

"Well, then, what do you think, sweetie-lumkins?" Flora said. "Would you enjoy seeing a bit of how the high and mighty live?"

Chou-Chou blinked and went back under the blanket, and Flora nodded. She was happy to find the duke seemed to be taking these strange events seriously. It made *her* wonder about it all, too, and feel a glimmer of hope that she might decipher it all before word got out and those new appointments turned to cancellations because she couldn't control her spirits. Where could those blasted diamonds be? Was it really the old duke who wanted them, or just someone far more corporeal trying to be clever? How could she even begin to find out who or why?

She glanced at the stack of well-read penny dreadfuls

on her bedside table. *Lady Arabella's Peril. The Bloody Hand of Fate.* Maybe she just had to follow the examples of the heroines in those tales. Follow the trail of clues before they led her off a cliff. But those stories always had their clues neatly lined up, like breadcrumbs on a floor before Mrs. Gibbs got to them. Ghosts were much more chaotic.

At least a glimpse of the old duke's papers might give her a start. There was just one problem. What on earth was a girl supposed to wear for a good snoop around a ducal house?

~

As Flora gazed up at the facade of Everton House just off Green Park, trying not to let her mouth gape open, she thought maybe she had chosen her ensemble all wrong. The sea-green and cream walking suit, one of her most subdued ensembles aside from her madame gowns, seemed just—too, too much.

A carriage rolled past in the lane behind her, carrying a young lady in pale blue taffeta edged in shimmery gray braid, a tip-tilted feathered hat perched on her glossy auburn hair, a gray silk parasol held daintily in a lace-gloved hand. *That* was the sort of dress Flora needed. But such a simple, elegant ensemble would cost far more than the number of clients she possessed could ever pay, and it was no good pining. She looked as fine as she could, and if the duke didn't like it he could stuff it! She was here to help him, after all. No one needed a cranky grandfather from beyond the grave putting a spoke in the wheels of marriage plans on top of lost jewels.

She tucked Chou-Chou, who seemed uncharacteristically quiet, as if she, too, didn't quite know what to make of her surroundings, more firmly under her arm and marched up the gleaming marble steps. The dark green-painted front door boasted a brass knocker in the shape of a roaring lion's head, and she pounded on it with far more confidence than she felt. She squared her shoulders, tilted up her chin, and pasted on her most dazzling smile. She hadn't been lead chorus girl (*with* lines to say) at the Follies for nothing.

The door opened, and the most intimidating man she had ever seen appeared. He was just the sort of butler she could imagined at Buck Palace. Tall, cadaverously thin, narrow-eyed, with a beaky nose just perfect for staring down at people over. Her smile threatened to falter a bit. She managed to hold onto it, though. Show business was show business, even at Green Park.

"Yes?" he said, the one little word seemingly drawn into multiple syllables.

"I am Madame Flora Flowerdew, calling on the Duke of Everton," she said, giving Chou-Chou a warning jostle as she started to growl. She used her other hand to hold out the card that came with duke's letter. "I have an appointment."

"Indeed?" He peered, even more narrow-eyed, at the card, as if he suspected a forgery. At last he nodded and stepped back. "Do come in, Madame—Flowerdew, was it? I shall ascertain if His Grace is at home."

Flora marched inside, and had to try not to gape all over again at the foyer. It was all black and white marble, chilly and vast, the curving staircase with its gilded balustrade and Axminster carpet soaring upward past alabaster plinths holding tall Chinese blue and white vases filled with lilies and carnations that scented the cold air. A glass dome high overhead cast down beams of grayish light, illuminating the disapproving faces in portraits hung on marble and silk-papered walls. It was like a museum, or a particularly posh bank, not like a home at all. No wonder the old duke was so ill-tempered.

"Do follow me," the butler said when he reappeared, his footsteps silent even on that tiled floor. He led her up and up those stairs, past more portraits, past Canova sculptures, through a doorway on a landing. "If you will wait here, madame."

As the door shut behind her, Flora let out the breath she was holding, and put Chou-Chou down on the thick, grass-green carpet. She toddled off to sniff at a potted palm, and gave a great sneeze. She shook her tawny head as if in disgust.

"I agree, sweetest. It could definitely use a bit of refurbishing." Flora doubted she had been shown into one of Everton House's grander chambers. It was dark and quite outdated, with maroon-red wallpaper that matched the heavy brocade draperies that cut out most of the light from the windows. A dark red porphyry mantelpiece carved with hideous faces stared at her, and she stuck her tongue out at them.

She drew off her gloves and wandered around the dim space, examining the palms in their brass pots (needed water, as well as a good going-over with Mrs. Gibbs' feather duster) and the bookshelves with their faded leather-bound covers. Ancient Greeks mostly, clearly unread. A painting of a storm-tossed galleon hung over the fireplace, not exactly cheering things up.

Two portraits hung on the maroon walls, a man and woman Flora realized must be the late duke and his duchess. The lady was definitely the same one she saw in Evie's photograph, just older, her dark hair silvery at the edges, her midnight blue satin gown more recent, a different tiara and brooch, but with the same basilisk stare. And the man, portly, bewhiskered, glaring, looked just the sort to rough up over some lost jewels.

"Quite ghastly, isn't it?" a voice said. Flora whirled around, her heart jittering, and saw the duke—the new, handsome one, of course, not the ghost—in the doorway. He'd been so quiet she hadn't heard him come in at

30

all. So much for being always on her guard in this cold house.

And she knew she really needed to be on her guard. He was still much too handsome for a girl's own good, with that golden hair glowing in the gloomy dimness, that rueful smile on his face as he looked around his own room.

"It's not exactly in the latest fashion," she said. "But if you like it..."

"I do not." He turned to the butler, who was hovering suspiciously. "Tea, please, Makepeace. And some water for little..." He glanced at Chou-Chou, who seemed to be munching a palm leaf.

"Chou-Chou," Flora said, trying unobtrusively to snatch the snack from the Pomeranian.

"Water for Madame Chou-Chou." He glanced around the room, taking in the bookshelves, the unfortunate plants, his glaring grandparents. "This room, this whole house really, is very much my grandfather's doing, I'm afraid. Just like Thornhill Abbey."

Flora ran a gloved fingertip over the draperies. Dusty. "You should call in Monsieur Balliard. I read he's the best decorator in London, he did the drawing room at Marlborough House. All slap up to the minute."

He laughed, and Flora couldn't help but notice he looked a bit different from when he stormed into her flat. Not as worried, maybe, younger. Maybe he, unlike her, had a good night's sleep. "He is also the most expensive decorator, I fear. And my grandfather, for all his, er, virtues, didn't really have over-full coffers in the end."

So was that why he had to marry Maud Petrie so urgently? Flora was sympathetic, to be sure. But also a bit disappointed. "Oh. Well. A bit of white paint and some new draperies, blue maybe, or cream, would do wonders." She thought of the fashionable girl in the carriage. "Or pearl gray! And maybe a touch of water for those plants."

31

"Quite right you are, Miss Flowerdew. I'm afraid I don't have the knack for housekeeping just yet." Two maids brought in tea trays, slightly tarnished silver that nevertheless held a delicious-looking array of sandwiches and pink-iced cakes. It seemed Everton House still had a good cook, no matter what. "I've been trying to keep up with the accounts since I inherited the title."

The maids curtsied and left the room, casting Flora curious glances. "You seem to have some maids who could do a bit of dusting. And there are plenty of warehouses in Cheapside that would be reasonable. They'd love to let clients know they supplied a ducal house. Might impress the Petries a bit." She poured out the tea and passed him a cup.

"Ah, you see, Miss Flowerdew, that is another reason I need to marry soon."

"A lady's touch around the house?"

He gave another little smile, one that made her stomach flip-flop just a bit. She distracted herself with one of those pretty cakes. "And because, if I am being honest, she has the purse to take to those warehouses. I got a note this morning saying Miss Petrie is too upset by all the strange events of late to receive me today."

"I'm surprised her parents allowed that. They do seem eager to find a way forward." She handed another cake to Chou-Chou, and shivered as she remembered those chaotic events in her séance chamber. "Though truly, if I could I would go under my blankets and not come out, too. It was rather frightening."

He gave her a concerned frown. "You do not strike me as a lady who is easily frightened, Miss Flowerdew."

"I'm not. Can't afford to be. But your grandfather did sound very angry."

He sat back in his chair, his foot tapping on the carpet, sending up a little dust cloud. "You think it *was* my grandfather, then?"

"I don't know. I can't really imagine who else would

be doing such a thing. The only people there were the Petries, and my maid Mary, and she's as honest as the day is long. We lock the front door when séance clients are there." She remembered Maud Petrie and her tearful pleas to stop the ducal match, but she decided not to mention that for now. "I do know I can't let it go on. A ghost in a séance is all well and good, but not one who is so unsatisfied with the customer service. And I can't have the Petries telling their friends not to come to me! I rely on good word of mouth." And she was pushing thirty now, too old to go back on the stage. That was for certain.

"I quite understand. The Petries wouldn't want any scandal, either."

"Would it be quite like your grandfather to behave like that?" Flora glanced at the portrait of the old man, who seemed to glower at her. She knew he would.

"Certainly. He was an absolute tartar. It was a relief to go off to school, despite the cold baths and Latin, and all that endless cricket. And he did seem to have an obsession with the diamonds. Maybe if we could really find them..."

We. Flora's heart fluttered all over again. "Then maybe the old tarter would be at peace, or at least the Petries would think he was. Or whoever is pulling an earthly prank would settle down."

"Hopefully so, yes. Grandfather did have rather a lot of people with reasons to dislike him. I've been sorting through his papers, as I wrote to you." He gestured toward a table at the other end of the room, its surface covered with boxes and ledgers.

Flora went to glance over them, her heart sinking at the sheer amount, the haphazardness of it all. It seemed no one in the Everton household believed in organization. "Oh, heavens," she whispered, and wished that butler had brought in something stronger than tea.

"Yes. Just so." Benedict came to her side and poked

his finger at a crooked stack of crumbling papers. They tumbled down into a chokingly dusty heap. "He did keep almost everything. Except letters from my father, that is. There are very few of those left. He was a disgrace to the Everton name, you see, running off and getting himself killed like that. And not many from my uncle. My grandfather didn't like him much, either, which I think is lucky for him as he could have a useful career, though he might not see it that way. Everything else is here, every note, every bill. Just not in any order."

"Well," Flora said briskly, and unpinned her hat. "Organization is one of my talents. The sooner we dive in, the sooner we might have some answers. Could that terrifying butler of yours be persuaded to bring us some brandy, Your Grace? And maybe some more of those lovely cakes."

He gave her an admiring glance. "I am quite sure he could. And, if we are going to wade into this horrible mess together, Miss Flowerdew, you should really call me Benedict."

Flora laughed. Benedict. Yes, it did suit him better than duke. She gave his hand a little shake, his touch warm, slightly callused, inviting. Too inviting. "And I'm Flora. Pleased to meet you." She sat down at the cluttered table, reached for a ledger, and sighed.

"Disorganized" proved to be a bit of an understatement. Flora shook her head as she studied a bill for Court robes for Queen Victoria's coronation in 1838, and laid it into the "finances, not relevant" box. At least they did have individual boxes now; letters to and from family, threats (also to and from family), threats from strangers (overflowing). Unfortunately, quite a few of the irate missives were from deceased authors. More recent ones went into their own receptacle. It would take a month of Sundays seances to contact all the dead letter writers. Flora tried to get Chou-Chou to sniff some of them and see if the pup's psychic intuition might be helpful, but C-C just blinked and went back to sleep under the table.

Flora took a sip of brandy, patted Chou-Chou's head, and reached for a battered old portfolio. It cracked when she opened it, and a few photographs and musty-lilac-scented letters tumbled out.

She picked up the top image. It was a girl on a trapeze, her pretty, dimpled faces smiling under a cloud of dark hair. Flora studied her costume of spangled tulle and tights with admiration. "Who is this?"

Benedict glanced at it, and his cheeks flushed a rather adorable pink. "That's my grandfather's, er, special friend. Mabel Bracknell. The Melodious Mabel, she was called. She used to sing on the trapeze, back when she was in the Astonishing Anderson's Imperial Circus. I think she retired a long time ago, though."

Flora studied the girl's statuesque figure, and realized she had a rather higher opinion of the old duke now. Melodious Mabel seemed quite a prize. The men at the Follies would have been fighting over her. "My, my. That dirty devil, your grandfather. I wouldn't have thought he followed the Prince of Wales's example."

"I hope he can't hear you say that. He despised the Marlborough House Set and all their scandalous doings. Said they were taking us right back to the Gory Georgians. That old hypocrite." He reached for the photograph. "I met her once, when I was a child. Backstage at the circus. She smelled of lilac powder, and gave me bonbons. I thought her rather nice, not terrifying like my grandmother." He turned over another photograph, the same woman but this time in a pale satin evening gown and ropes of pearls big as eggs. "I guess she had her reasons for putting up with him."

Flora laughed. Anyone might, for pearls like that. "Is she still alive?"

"As far as I know. I think I heard she retired to Brighton or something."

Flora poured out more brandy for them both and took up some letters. "How odd. Could he have actually given some of the diamonds to Mabel? Or promised them to her?"

"I wouldn't have thought so, he was such a stickler for title and position. But listen to this! She calls him 'honey-bear sweetums.' I suppose anyone could get soppy for a pair of spangled tights."

Flora giggled. "I do like a bit of soppy. It makes me like the old tartar a bit more, if he was a honey-bear. I think we need to find Miss Bracknell, and see what her story is." The gilded clock on the mantel chimed the hour, and she glanced up, startled. Time had quite flown by while she was elbow-deep in dusty letters, and it hadn't even been dull. Not with Benedict beside her. "Is that the time? I need to fly!"

"An important appointment?"

"Oh, yes. Old Miss Russell. She keeps begging her long-late mother to say where she hid the silver chocolate pot, but no word yet."

"It seems like you have lots of mysteries in your life."

She reached for her hat and gloves, and roused Chou-Chou from his nap. "Oh, dukie, you don't know the half of it." She pinned on her hat, rather hoping she could stay there with him, even in that hideous room. "You try to find Melodious Mabel, and I'll visit Miss Petrie this week and try to set up another séance. Maybe one of them knows more than they've said..."

Five

In the end, they didn't even have to go all the way to Brighton to find Mabel Bracknell after all. Apparently she had gone through her retirement savings in double-quick time and gone back to the circus life. She was now the wardrobe mistress at the Royal York Circus, currently residing at the Hyde Hippodrome near the Thames. So of course there was nothing to do but take an evening at the circus.

Flora and Benedict were told by the terrifyingly huge guard, in no uncertain terms, that Miss Bracknell couldn't possibly have visitors before the show. There were dozens of people to dress, don'cha know. They just had to take a box and watch the performance first.

How absolutely dreadful, Flora thought in complete delight as she settled onto a red velvet-cushioned gilt chair and gazed around the crowded amphitheater. It had been simply ages since she went to the circus; she usually had to run the circuses in her séance room instead. The laughing crowd, the sparkling lights, the scent of peanuts and ale and animals and greasepaint—it made her want to clap her gloved hands in delight.

"Isn't this just grand?" she said. "I used to love the circus when I was a kiddie. I would sneak in the back and hide under the risers." She didn't mention the fact that she had to crawl out of a cracked basement window at the orphanage to escape—or that she was beaten unmercifully about the legs when she was caught. The sparkle of the show had made it all worth it.

"I'm afraid this is my first time at the circus at all," Benedict said.

Flora glanced at him in surprised sympathy. "Your very first time? But I thought surely dukes could do as they like!"

He laughed, but it didn't sound entirely joking, and his eyes were shadowed. "You forget, I grew up with my grandparents, technically speaking anyway. After my father died, my mother was very sickly, she kept mostly to her rooms and didn't live long after him. I've always been rather surprised two such opposites, my traveling father and my homebound mama, made a match of it at all, but she *was* a marquess's daughter, and beautiful. She never had any say in my childhood at all, and my grandparents would never, ever have approved of a circus." He looked around, a smile forming on his lips. "It's marvelous, isn't it?"

"It certainly is." Flora fluffed at the ruffled skirt of her gown, one of her favorites, a creation of peachy-pink moire silk edged with beaded black lace. A bit much, maybe, for a circus, but she was very glad she had worn it now. She knew how fine she looked in it, and his smile when he looked at her made it worth it.

Then she remembered he was practically engaged.

She turned back to studying the ring through her opera glasses, taking in the trapezes waiting overhead, the laughing, excited crowd, ranging from jewel-draped ladies and their dark-suited escorts in the boxes to the middle-class families in the risers, and shabbier laborers in the high-up, cheap seats.

"Oh, I brought these," Benedict said, sounding almost shy. Flora turned to see he held out two enormous satin boxes, one filled with caramels, one with candied violet-topped chocolates. She recognized the name of the famous French confectionery printed on the be-bowed lids. Grateful séance patrons had once given her a small box, but she could never indulge in their wondrousness herself. "I wasn't sure which you would like, so I just got both."

"What a poppet you are! I love them all." What an ingrate that Maud Petrie was, Flora thought as she popped a violet cream into her mouth and sighed happily. Imagine not wanting to marry someone like this lovely man, diamonds or not. She took a caramel, too. "Which will you have?"

He leaned closer and said confidingly, "Do you know what I really want? Some of the peanuts that man over there is selling."

"Then you should have some! Right now."

"Should I?"

"You're the duke now! You get to eat what you like, I say."

As he dug merrily into his greasy paper cone of peanuts, the gaslights suddenly blazed brighter, and a wave of howls, stomping, and wild applause broke out. The ringmaster in his gold-braided red-coat glory, strode out and waved his top hat. "And now, our maestro of the fire baton, Fiery Freddie and his Efflorescent Females!" And much to Flora's delight, a swarm of fire-baton tossing acrobats flew into the ring.

They were followed by someone called Sybil the Songbird, trilling as she soared above the crowd on a flower-wrapped trapeze much like Mabel must have once done. Flora went through the chocolates as they watched a knife-thrower nearly impale a spangle and feathers-clad assistant, and equestrian show of dancing horses, Chinese acrobats tumbling and contorting, dancers, prancing poodles led by girls in fluffy white tulle short skirts, all circling the rings like dervishes. It was all quite dizzying, and Flora nearly forgot she was actually meant to be working.

Until she happened to glance up from a juggler, and saw a rather familiar figure in a box just opposite. It was only for an instant, as the spotlight danced across it, but she was sure it was Maud Petrie. Dressed in a daring gown of marigold-yellow silk, laughing and happy in a way completely different from the weepy girl in Flora's séance room—and holding hands with a bespectacled young man.

Flora blinked, and the boxes were in deep shadows again. She glanced at Benedict, but he didn't appear to have noticed anything, he was so occupied with his peanuts and the jugglers. Flora wondered if indeed Miss Petrie had been the one to sabotage the séance somehow, to use the angry dead duke to persuade her parents she couldn't possibly marry Everton. If she had, Flora's admiration for her soared.

When the show was over, in a glorious twirl of horses, dogs, acrobats tumbling, music blasting away, Flora tried to find Miss Petrie but she had vanished into the crowd. Flora and Benedict made their way back to the stage door, still guarded by that giant. He was calmly cleaning his fingernails with a dagger point.

"Got to keep up the grooming. Ladies like it," he said, examining what Flora had to admit was a nice manicure. "You two back to see Mabel, then? I dunno why. She's a bordy old lady."

As Flora watched, Benedict seemed to magically put on a "duke face," just as if he was performing in the circus. The youthful, eager, funny man who gobbled peanuts became haughty and chilly, his cheekbones and jaws even seeming sharper, his eyes icier. "She was a friend of a relation of mine. The Duke of Everton."

The giant snickered, but he did step back and even

gave a little bow. "Was she now? Must have been a long time ago. Well, go on in."

They made their way through the narrow, tiny corridors of backstage, past dressing rooms and prop stores. It all took Flora right back to the days before Madame Flowerdew, the smell of sweat and greasepaint and rosin, the shouts and laughter, the glitter that stuck to her shoes. She remembered so well rushing along just such halls, adjusting feathers in her hair, dodging stagehands' pinching fingers, her legs aching and head pounding.

She shook her head, clearing away those old days, those old ways of doing and rushing and thinking. It was done now. She had a different job, her own home, a proper life. But it could all go away if she didn't find those wretched diamonds.

The wardrobe room was vast, windowless, filled with racks of feathered and ruffled costumes, cracked mirrors, rows of worn-out dance shoes. A woman stood at the far end, her brown hair threaded with gray, her shoulders stooped in her plain black dress, her hands flying as she tsked over a torn tulle skirt. "These girls! No thought for anyone as has to mend their carelessness, no respect these days."

"Mrs. Bracknell?" Benedict said.

She looked up with a surprised frown. It had indeed been a long time since her days as Mabel the Melodious. Her cheeks were deeply creased as dried apples, her eyebrows like caterpillars. But they crawled above eyes still the beautiful color of melted caramels. "Who wants to know, then?"

Benedict took out one of his cards. "I am the Duke of Everton, and this is Miss Flowerdew."

Mabel's shriveled mouth opened in an astonished "o" as she looked at the engraved card. "Johnny's boy? I thought he died off in some desert or some such."

Flora nearly laughed aloud to think of that fearsome dead duke as "Johnny."

41

"I am his son, and he died in Cornwall," Benedict said.

"Oh, yes. Don't have much of a look about him, do you? Your grandfather, I mean." She went back to hemming at the tulle. "Whadya want, then, after all this time?"

"I understand you were good friends with my grandfather."

Mabel gave a harsh laugh, and poured out a measure of gin from a flask hidden in her workbox. "You could say that, sure enough. He was a sweet old duck, really. Most couldn't see that."

"I can imagine that," Benedict muttered.

Mabel suddenly scowled, and took a gulp of the gin. "He didn't do right by me in the end, though. Not at all."

"That may have something to do with the reason for our visit," Flora said, putting on some of her former Follies accent in an attempt to reassure the understandably suspicious Mabel. "Men can be such swine. In what way did he not do right by you?"

Mabel sighed and dropped the tulle, a faraway look in her still-lovely eyes. "He'd always been a generous sort. Not the most lavish; I'd known better. But solid-like. He used to say 'Mabel, don't you worry about a thing later, I have a fine gift in mind that'll see you through.' And then, nothing. I had to give up my Brighton flat! Come back here with these bloody fools." She kicked at the torn skirt.

"What sort of gift was that?" Flora asked.

Mabel swallowed the last of her gin and poured out more. "It was a secret, see. The duchess couldn't find out. He was going to give me a diamond."

Flora and Benedict exchanged a startled glance. "A diamond?" Flora said.

"Oh, he gave me some nice jewels, but he said this one would be different. Special. Fit for a duchess, even."

42

Mabel gave a bark of laughter. "More fool me. I never saw such a thing. Could have really used it, too. After all I did for him."

"And you never thought of just taking what you were owed?" Benedict asked.

Mabel narrowed her eyes on him. "Steal, you mean? Well, dukie sir, I might have just been a trapeze girl, but I weren't no thief. I just took him at his word." She looked down at the dusty floor for a long, silent moment, tracing a needle-reddened finger around the edge of her flask. Flora had the distinct sense she was not telling them quite everything. Could she have helped herself to the diamonds? Been in league with Benedict's father against her duke, or maybe duped both of them?

But then what had happened to the stones between then and now? Mabel would have had to be very clever to steal them, but seemingly not clever enough to profit by it.

Mabel sipped more gin, sunk in her own memories and clearly not going to say more any time soon. Benedict took Flora's arm and led her out into the corridor, quieter now that the show was long over.

"What do you think?" he said, dodging around a stray poodle.

"I'm not sure." Flora told him her thoughts, the possibilities of the past, the obvious reality of Mabel's present, and he nodded.

"She doesn't seem to be a criminal mastermind jewel thief," he agreed. "Yet I suppose one never knows. Surely a true thief is smart enough not to *look* like one."

"You'd be surprised how stupid most criminals really are," Flora said. She remembered a woman who poisoned her husband for his bank account, then hid the poison in a cocoa tin right by the bed. "We really can't completely discount her yet, but why would she be here? Why not some cozy villa in the South of France?"

"Like my grandmother, you mean?"

43

"So that's where the dowager duchess lives?"

"Oh, yes. In the Villa d'Or near Cannes, with fifty servants and three carriages. Also an army of Pekingese who aren't nearly as smart as your Chou-Chou."

Flora nodded. Chou-Chou did hate Pekingese. "But I thought your family coffers were low? Thus the Petries."

Benedict grimaced. "So they are. I know her dower was not large, but she's been living there ever since my grandfather died. Said the dower house in the village near Thornhill was too tiny."

"Maybe there *is* a criminal mastermind at large, then. But it's not your grandfather's mistress." She remembered the photograph in Evie's office, the dowager duchess in full diamond-blazing glory with her flinty stare. Flora wouldn't put a bit of jewel thievery past her.

Benedict laughed. "My grandmother is no fool, true. But I haven't seen her in ages. She never comes back to England. Do you think a quick jaunt across the Channel would be worth our while?"

Flora stared up at him, struck by that use of *our*. She would so love to see France! Especially with him beside her, his arm under her hand, his quirk of a smile. The feeling she had with him of being a true lady. But it would never do to get too close. She refused to let her heart get broken and interfere with the life she worked so hard to build.

Still—France...

"I do think no one would find it odd for you to call on your grandmother."

They reached the backstage door leading outside, no nail-filing guard in sight now. "Then who should we question next?"

Flora thought Maud Petrie, laughing in her circus box. If it *was* Maud. She needed to be sure. "I'll work on setting up that séance we talked about, with your fiancée's family. They surely might know more than

44

they're saying. Or maybe your grandfather could make another appearance and explain himself!"

"Or maybe the Petries *are* being my grandfather, for some odd reason. Is it very hard to counterfeit spirits?"

"I will have you know, I am a genuine medium!" Flora surreptitiously crossed her gloved fingers. "But I do read things, and it can be a tricky thing, but if you know what you're doing its possible."

"I doubt Maud could do that, she seems so sweet and kind."

So he actually liked Maud Petrie. Loved her? What would knowing she went to the circus with someone else do to him? Flora found she didn't want him hurt, not if it could be helped. "Her father, though..."

Benedict grinned. "Yes. Sir Henry. He does seem most intent on one day being grandfather to a duke. Yet I'm already prepared to marry his daughter. Why would he make such a fuss?"

"For the right of his daughter to wear that tiara? I'd fight for that. But it's hard to say, since I don't know the Petries at all well. The first I heard of them was when Miss Petrie, Sir Henry's sister, wrote to set up the séance. She said they wanted your family's blessing or some such thing." Flora glimpsed a tent near the gates of the hippodrome grounds, with a sign over the striped silk doorway. *Madame Voronova, Tarot Card Reader.* "Perhaps the cards might know!"

He followed her gaze, and frowned doubtfully. "Tarot cards?"

"Yes. Sometimes they can show us things we can't quite see on our own yet. Come on, it couldn't hurt anything." And it would mean she could spend a little more time with him. Despite the sad necessity of questioning the pitiful Mabel Bracknell, it had actually been a rather pleasant evening. Fun, even. She grabbed his hand and tugged him toward the tent.

As they slipped through the silk streamers of the

45

entrance, Flora had to blink for a moment to clear the dark haze. The round space, hung with more streamers of burnt orange and crimson, was laid with a faded rug woven with signs of the zodiac. Large, embroidered cushions were scattered about, but the only furniture was an oval table spread with a red cloth and two carved chairs. The only light was a branch of candles on the table, sputtering low. The air smelled of flowery incense. From one professional to another, Flora had to applaud the stage set.

"Welcome," a low, creaking, vaguely Russian voice said. "You have come to seek Madame Voronova's help?"

Flora blinked again into the shadows, and saw a tiny woman seated behind the table, her red turban barely visible above the enormous crystal ball resting there on a wrought silver base. The face below the bright silk folds was round as a peach, surprisingly young and sweet and dimpled. But the dark brown eyes, bright as snapdragon raisins, were shadowed.

Madame V held out a heavily beringed hand. "Come, don't be shy. Is it the wisdom of the crystal you seek?"

Shy was a word no one had ever used to describe Flora. And usually such gimcrackery would be enough to entirely put her off. Yet there was something, some *feeling*, about that tent. She couldn't quite put her finger on it. A certain clammy feeling, creeping, like tentacles, holding her fast. But there was no time to be a goose, not in her business. She marched forward and sat down in the chair across from Madame Voronova. Benedict stood silently behind her.

Madame V's eyes flickered indifferently over him, unlike most women's would, before they settled on Flora. "*Nyet*," she murmured. "I think it's the cards for you. Your heart is much too tumultuous for the crystal today."

46

She handed Flora the cards to shuffle them, imparting her energy to the pasteboard squares, before Madame took them back and laid them out. She frowned as she studied them.

"Hmm, the fool," she said, "the most vulnerable of the cards, unaware of life's magnitudes sometimes, of his own strength and potential. You should embrace what lies ahead, you are strong enough to endure them. And here—The High Priestess. The teacher of magic. If you want the benefits of or knowledge, you must trust and cooperate in spirit."

Flora and Benedict exchanged a glance. "Trust my grandfather?" he said doubtfully.

Madame V. shrugged. "I only read what is here. I do not know your grandfather." She tapped another card. "Perhaps this is your grandfather, no? The Emperor reversed. Tyrannical, preferring his own version of events to what is true."

Benedict laughed. "I think your card there does not lie, madame."

"They never do." She studied another one, two partners entwined. "Ah, the lovers. Crossroads, choices to be made." She smiled slyly at Flora. "I think you, mademoiselle, have never really been in love. It can be a great challenge to all of us. A great challenge to trust, no?"

"Love is not necessary to a good life," Flora answered. "In fact, I have seen it too often stand in the way of happiness."

Madame studied her closely for a long moment, making her fidget. "I sense things about people. You have armor around your heart, thick and thorny. It may protect you, but it also limits you."

Flora was suddenly all too aware of Benedict at her side, so close, so warm. Could he find the chink in that armor? She hoped not.

"And Death," Madame whispered, turning over a card painted with a fearsome hooded figure. "He scythes

47

the cord that links us to the past, liberates us to go forward without fear. But when he is reversed like this..." She shook her head. "It is not yet time for the cord to be cut. You must beware. Danger lies ahead." She slumped back in her chair. "You must go. I can tell you no more."

"But..." Flora protested, wanting, *needing* to know more.

"Go!" Madame V cried, and Flora ran out of the tent.

"Let me find us a hansom," Benedict said. Flora could feel his worry as he watched her, feel it in his protective hand on her elbow as they turned away from the now-darkened hippodrome onto the busier lanes. She didn't need him, or want him, to worry about her; she'd been on her own for such a very long time. But, oh, it did feel rather nice. Was this how it was to be a real lady? To feel cushioned from the arrows of the world? To know a hand was always waiting there to catch you?

It was lovely. *Too* lovely. She couldn't afford to get used to it. She'd worked too hard to build a strong carapace around herself.

Flora drew her arm away and strode ahead, twitching her fine moire skirts away from a man casting up his accounts into the gutter. "No hansom yet, dukie. I could use a breath of fresh air." She took a deep breath, and inhaled coal dust and crushed flowers. "As fresh as we can get, anyway."

They walked for a while in silence along the embankment of the river, the lights of the city twinkling around them like a jewel box, giggling couples ducking into the shadows, chattering crowds exiting the theaters nearby. Sometimes, Flora actually rather liked London, the sheer life and variety and color of it. When she didn't loathe it.

Once they reached a stone bridge that looked down at the darkened river, Flora stared out over the water, that silvery ribbon of ever-winding, ever-shifting tides that strangely always seemed the same in the always changing city. Maybe the only thing that *did* seem the same. A boat drifted past, the figures like silhouettes in the night.

She felt Benedict standing close to her, his elbows leaning on the stone balustrade as he, too, watched the river, his tawny hair tousled and in the moonlight. She couldn't help but lean just a little closer to his warmth.

"What did she mean, the card reader?" he said. "When she said the cord is not ready to be cut."

Flora tossed him what she hoped was a careless smile. "Not familiar with the ways of the tarot, then?"

He laughed. "I did have a nanny once who claimed she could read fortunes in cards, but she used decks of Happy Families. And sometimes made us play Racing Demon with her."

"And what was your fortune?"

"Great riches, as I'm sure they tell everyone. And love."

Flora giggled in spite of herself. "Well, Madame Voronova implied armor lies around the heart."

Benedict gave a scoffing, funny little snort. "That sounds a bit unlikely."

"As unlikely as a dead duke getting angry about his lost diamonds?"

"Too true, Miss Flowerdew." He rubbed at his jaw thoughtfully. She noticed a few golden whiskers were appearing there, and she wondered fleetingly, silly-like, how they might feel against her own cheek. "This has been quite the most unusual week of my life."

"Mine, too," she murmured.

"Has it really? I would have thought you'd seen all kinds of fascinating things in the séance line of work."

"A thing or two, maybe." But not in her séances. Those were usually about missing cats or people wanting to know where auntie had stashed the silver, or, sadly, if a husband had really loved his bereaved wife.

49

People just needed a bit of reassurance then, someone to listen, and Flora was good at that. She'd had to learn to do that since she was a toddler, to sense what people around her were feeling. All the main events—those happened before she put out her medium-ship shingle.

She glanced up at the man who stood beside her, so handsome, so strong, so easygoing in his confidence. How could he really begin to understand what Florrie Grubbins had seen?

"I've never run around London chasing diamonds before, though, all on some ghost's say-so," she said lightly. "But I think you and I are both sensible sorts, dukie."

"I'd like to think I am. And I'm quite sure you are."

"Thank you. So, as sensible people, we have to say ghosts don't exist."

"I certainly would have said so."

"Then what is causing these events? Who else knows about those diamonds? And why did I feel that odd way in Madame Voronova's tent? I felt so—well, trapped, I suppose. Menaced."

"That was what you made feel faint?" he said gently.

She smiled ruefully. "Now you see my secret. I am a beastly coward."

"Now that I will never believe!"

"Oh, yes! I would run a mile if you asked me to ride a horse, those giant, smelly beasts. But ghosts..." She shook her head.

"Did you recognize Madame Voronova at all?"

"Not a bit. Could she be working with someone, in league to find the diamonds? Miss Petrie, even?" After all, Maud *had* been at the circus.

"Possible, I suppose, but as you said, Miss Petrie doesn't quite seem the criminal mastermind type."

"One never knows! They are mostly pretty bacon-brained, but there was one I met who robbed the whole glove counter at Bon Marche quite blind." Flora smiled in remembered admiration. "Beautifully done, that was. And I think maybe we'll find this proves to be the same —the work of some human, not a spirit."

"I agree, but which one? So many people did hate my grandfather, and admired the diamonds."

Flora sighed to think of how true that was. No one seemed to have really liked the man, not his son, not his wife, not his mistress, not his peers and business associates and servants. Sad, really. "I really should go home and read through more of those old letters we found. Perhaps you could visit that old butler of yours. Talbot, right? If he can be found."

"Not a problem, I think his great-niece is housekeeper's assistant at Thornhill Abbey now. I'll write to her in the morning. Perhaps I should come back to the circus, as well? See if there's some link between Madame Voronova and—well, anyone."

He looked so eager, Flora wondered if what he really wanted was another glimpse of that winsome poodle wrangler in her fluffy tutu. Ah, well, not really her business. More was the pity. "A good idea. I might visit another medium, too."

"Ask her for more tricks of the trade?"

"Something of the sort." Flora remembered Edith Evans (aka Madame Edie Duvall), a well-known psychic she had met once at a tea party. Edie had been in the business for many years, and knew positively everyone in the trade. "I know someone who does have an amazing talent, though it's not really in chatting with ghosts. She just has enormous intuition of the thoughts of others, their emotions and reactions. That's what a good medium does, really. Senses the needs and fears of others. She is also quite kind and reassuring, so might have some valuable advice."

Flora tapped her closed fan against her gloved palm. From being on the stage, she herself had found such intuition invaluable—it had saved her more than once

51

from foul-breathed backstage mashers. But she wasn't nearly as gifted as Edie.

She glanced over at Benedict again, and he looked thoughtful, distant in the moonlight. She wished she had such intuition when it came to *him*. As handsome and genial and well-bred as he was, she had a tiny glimmer of something going on just underneath.

"I really should be getting home," she said. "I think we should find that hansom now..."

Once back in her quiet flat, Flora made herself some cocoa, plaited her hair, and wrapped up in her old quilted dressing gown, careful not to wake Mary. She wanted to let the fun and lights of the circus percolate in her mind just a little longer, before the dark menace in the tarot tent took over again. And she definitely didn't want to think about Benedict.

She sat down at her desk with Chou-Chou on a cushion at her feet, and studied the tall piles of the old duke's letters and papers Benedict had sent over. She sighed to be faced with such a sea of crabbed, faded, musty and yellowed pages, but someone had to do it. She took a gulp of cocoa, and dove in.

An hour later, she sighed again and thought she quite loathed that old duke even more. Berating servants, quarreling with his wife, threatening all the time to disown his son, suing his neighbors. He also wouldn't pay what he owed to tradesmen. She put aside a thick stack of begging letters from unfortunate vintners, tailors, chandlers, plasterers, and jewelers—but no one involving diamonds.

At the bottom of the pile was a very well-worn, long message spotted as if tears had fallen onto it. It was edged with black, and signed "Mrs. Elfrida Alexander Stillworth, Widow, Mysore, India."

So the old miser had been cruel to colonial widows, too. That figured, Flora thought. She reached for a small quizzing glass and tried to decipher the faded ink. It was a sad tale, one of poverty and despair, of love lost, a child worried over, diamonds sold but not fully paid for. Sold to the duke.

Flora sat back in her chair. The diamonds hadn't come straight to the duke from some maharajah, then. They had belonged to this Stillworth family. An impoverished family, it seemed, a widow with a child. And the duke hadn't fully paid the family for the stones. No wonder he was cursed.

Flora wondered if this child ever did visit the duke, and what happened. She rather hoped he cleaned the duke's clock but good. There were no more letters from Mrs. Stillworth, widow, to tell her the rest of the story. Maybe Evie could find something in her newspaper archives, if the dates could match up. It looked like the duke must have been fairly young when Mrs. Alexander wrote to him.

Flora carefully tucked away the letter in a locked cubbyhole, and drank the last of her cocoa. Chou-Chou had gone away to snuggle under the bedclothes, and Flora gratefully went to join her. It had been rather a long day, and her old dancing feet ached, but when she closed her eyes she felt again that cold, clammy, creeping dark menace that crept over her in that tent. Had to followed her home? Was *she* cursed now, too, just by hearing about those bloody diamonds?

She sat up, shaking, and re-lit the bedside candle. Chou-Chou blinked out at her, confused, yet seemed to recognize something was really amiss. She sat up, shook out her caramel-colored fur, and clambered up onto Flora's lap to lick her chin.

Flora closed her eyes and held onto the dog tightly, trying to force away that chilling panic. She hadn't felt that way in a very long time, and there was surely no reason for it now. She wasn't Florrie Grubbins anymore. She was safe.

She laid back on the pillows, and Chou-Chou snuggled beside her. Yes, she was safe now—and she was going to keep herself that way, one way or another.

Six

"Oooh, lots in the post today, Miss Flora!" Mary said merrily, *too* merrily for Flora's taste considering *some* people had only two hours sleep. Mary drew back the curtains with a great swoosh, and plopped down the tray, which did indeed hold lots of letters as well as tea and toast.

Flora groaned. But the day was going to wear on whether she liked it or not, and those diamonds were never going to find themselves. Chou-Chou buried deeper under the blankets, but Flora couldn't. She reached for the letters as Mary gathered up the moire gown and shook out its ruffles.

"Have a good time last night, then, miss?"

"Yes, I went to the circus." Flora desperately gulped down a whole cup of strong tea.

"Cor, I love the circus! Especially the tightropes. Was it ever so fun?"

"It was for work, I'm afraid." Flora closed her eyes for a moment, remembering the lights, the violet cream chocolates, the duke's delighted smile over his peanuts. "Parts of it *were* rather fun, though. We should go again, you and me, before they move on from the Hippodrome."

Mary grinned ecstatically. "Just fancy! Oh, once I thought I might run away with the circus myself. To do the equestrian act or some such. They had this magician, you see..." Her smile faded. "Didn't work out that way, though."

Flora just nodded. She didn't ask much about Mary's past; Mary didn't ask about hers. It was their useful system. "Then as soon as this case is finished, we will go. We'll even take a box." She buttered her toast, unable to face marmalade quite yet. "Mary, do you know any of the other maids around Town? Enough to get the best gossip?"

"I have a natter in the park sometimes with a few of them, sure enough. Anyone in particular?"

"It's rather long odds, but maybe someone who worked for the old Duke of Everton, or who might know a family called Stillworth who were out in India. Any tidbit you find, no matter how tiny, could be very helpful."

Mary smiled again. "Oooh, miss! Fancy me a detective. I'll get right on that. Oh, and I did talk to my friend Pete, as used to be a pickpocket around Everton House way. He can't remember no one picking up a haul like diamonds."

"Thank you so much, Mary. You are a peach." Feeling a bit revived after her tea, Flora sorted through the rest of the post. "Oh, good, the Petries have agreed to another séance! Sir Henry wants me to visit Maud to, er, give her a mature lady's sensible advice." She laughed, even though she didn't much care for that 'mature' business. "Imagine that, Mary—me, sensible!" Especially when Maud had a mother and an aunt under her own roof. She shouldn't need Flora's dubious counsel.

"Come on then, Miss Flora, you're no fool. I'd come to you for advice."

"I'm not sure I have much advice to give to a young

lady who doesn't seem to want to marry a duke." Especially a handsome, funny, sweet dukie like Benedict. But then, maybe her heart was already won by that bespectacled lad at the circus, and it was hard to argue with that. "But I'll go by the Petrie house before I drop in on Evie at the newspaper."

The next letter was a surprise. "You'll have to press my best frock, Mary! I'm off to dinner at the house of a duke's uncle tonight."

Mary gasped. "Is it a ball? That would be grand."

"I doubt it. Just the duke, his uncle and cousin, and the cousin's wife. It seems they would have been the heirs if Benedict's father hadn't married before he ran off to get himself killed." She wondered if they were still sore about all that. Probably; who wouldn't be? But sore enough to steal the jewels, and then kill the heir in a Cornwall cave?

Mary opened the wardrobe and sorted through the gowns hanging there. She pulled out an emerald green satin edged with buttercup tulle and diamante-sparkled silk roses. "What about this one?"

Flora remembered late, raucous suppers in her actress days, and shook her head. "We're not having supper in a back room with the Prince of Wales. The duke's cousin is some kind of respectable businessman in the City. Do we have anything a little—quieter?"

Mary frowned. To her, bright and elaborate was always better. She took out a mauve organdie edged with cream bows. "This? They do say this is the Princess of Wales's favorite color, so it must be stylish."

"Yes, perfect, Mary. And now something in gray, I think. I have to go tell a girl to quit being a silly goose and marry the duke already."

~

Larks, Flora thought as she studied the Petrie house on Bedford Square from beneath her blue lace parasol. She could see why a duke who had lost all his diamonds might like to ally himself with all this. It was at least four times the size of any other house on the square, gleaming white with bright blue trim, every window (and there were a *lot* of them) hung with satins and brocades. Blue and white pots overflowing with ivy lined the white marble steps. It was all crack up to the mark, unlike Everton House.

She knew those draperies might not be considered in the very best of taste by some old snobs, too bright, too many gold tassels, but she quite adored it all. She wondered if one of the second-hand dealers she knew might have some fringe just like that.

She sighed, and hoped that maybe an up-close look at the Petries' furnishings might be a bit of compensation for having to snoop into a young lady's private business. Digging about in the love affairs of others was always more interesting on the stage than in real life, where it all tended to get too messy and a bit boring.

She rang the bell pull, and assumed a suitably somber expression. She was meant to be Madame Flowerdew today, after all. Her wiggy was in place under a dark blue hat trimmed in striped gray ribbon, her walking suit more gray, her earrings plain pearl buttons. Talk about dull.

She felt a tiny prickle on the back of her neck, that sensation she got sometimes when someone was staring at her. Hoping desperately it wasn't the duke's ghost following her about, she glanced up and saw Miss Priscilla Petrie, Sir Henry's spinster sister, watching her from one of the upstairs windows. When she noticed Flora noticing, she ducked back behind the gold and maroon curtain again.

To Flora's surprise, Lady Petrie herself opened the door. Her plush figure was stylishly clad in a lavender silk and lace tea gown, her graying dark hair dressed high in curls, but her eyes were red-rimmed, her cheeks puffy. She seemed to sense that Flora was taken aback by the absence of grand butler as gatekeeper, because she grimaced, and waved her handkerchief in a helpless little gesture.

"Oh, Madame Flowerdew, it is so kind of you to call and see how we are faring after such a distressing experience," Lady Petrie said, beckoning Flora quickly into the foyer. "I was so touched to receive your note. And do forgive our lack of butler today. It seemed better to give the staff a day or two away. Servants can be such gossips."

"Indeed," Flora murmured, thinking of how much she loved a good natter with Mary over a whiskey.

Lady Petrie whispered, "We would never want anything to get in the way of dear Maudie's marital bliss."

Flora remembered "dear Maudie" laughing with someone not her future fiancé in the circus box, and nodded. "It seemed when you departed that Sir Henry was quite concerned. Has he, too, been having doubts about allying with such a family?"

Lady Petrie's jaw hardened. "Oh, Henry. He can be quite hideously superstitious, though you would never guess such a thing. I fear his parents were rather fusty old Presbyterian sorts, you see. My own dear father was a vicar. C of E, of course. Incumbent of a very good living in Shropshire. I was Miss Duff, then, and went to a very proper school as a girl, Miss Johnson's School for Clergyman's Daughters." She patted at her carefully curled hair. "My father would have had nothing to do with such notions as curses."

Flora remembered how Lady Petrie had seemed plenty frightened herself when the old duke was roaring at them. "Yes, of course. I do assure you we usually only see spirits of the gentlest sort when sitting in my circle."

59

"And I am sure the late duke can only have been a true gentleman in life! Like his grandson."

Now there Flora could agree with her. Despite his initial prickliness, Benedict *did* seem like a gentleman. Too much so. His grandfather, on the other hand... "And how does Miss Petrie fare today?"

"Terribly upset, I'm afraid. She is a sensitive soul. She takes after me." Lady Petrie glanced in an elaborate, gilt-framed mirror hanging above a marble pier table that held a huge, sneeze-inducing arrangements of lilies. She straightened the triple row of pearls at her throat. "She will make a lovely duchess. Which is why we can't let this nonsense continue! Diamonds can be bought, after all, we don't need those old ones. I could find her a much more fashionable design in any Bond Street shop. If only she and my husband would stop worrying about curses!"

Flora gently touched the lady's lace sleeve and smiled softly. "How can I be of assistance, then, Lady Petrie? I feel so terribly responsible."

Lady Petrie's face crumpled, and she dabbed at her eyes with her handkerchief. "I am so glad to know I have an ally, Madame Flowerdew! One can often feel so alone here, where my husband and daughter lack a—a clear vision. I am sure you can reassure them. Let them know that the late duke's message cannot have been malevolent."

Flora nearly laughed aloud. She thought Lady Petrie, as a good C of E goer, a vicar's daughter, wouldn't believe in ghostly curses. But then no one, not even Flora herself, knew at all *what* to believe right at that moment. "I'm afraid the spirits are unclear right now, but I know that together we can make things correct once more. May I speak with Miss Petrie?"

"Certainly, certainly! My husband is not at home, so now is the perfect moment." Lady Petrie led Flora through the foyer, so different from the austere elegance of Everton House with its layers of rugs on the parquet floors, its carved stands holding sculptures and potted plants, its crimson-striped wallpaper, and up a staircase of carved mahogany. Flora was happy it was indeed worth a look at the house. There were so many paintings, waxy things under glass, slipper chairs and hassocks, she was sure she could never take it all in. At the staircase landing was a bookcase with a locked glass front, lined with ancient-looking books. Maybe old tomes of necromancy and spells? That would be shocking indeed in such a very proper house! But no, it just seemed to be poetry and Dickens novels.

Maud's chamber was another story. All pink and white and silver, be-bowed and misty with tulle, gowns scattered on every chair and chaise, shoes piled on the pink and white flowered carpet, a dressing table covered every inch with perfume bottles and silver brushes and stacks of the same penny dreadful novels Flora herself enjoyed.

Maud lay on her side on one of the pink satin chaises, still clad in her dressing gown, her dark curls tousled around her pretty face. Like her mother, she had been crying, but she didn't try to hide it. Her peachy complexion was blotched, her eyes swollen. She blew her nose loudly into a crumpled handkerchief.

"Maudie, look who has come to call on us. It's Madame Flowerdew," Lady Petrie chirped. She bustled about the room, tossing open the pink silk curtains, picking up a discarded ribbon-edged petticoat.

Maud barely lifted her head from the cushion. She sniffled, and glanced at Flora with eyes wide with—was it fear? "Did she bring ghosts with her?"

"They don't usually follow me out of the circle," Flora said. "I was worried you might be frightened. I confess, I see rather odd things every week, but even I was taken aback."

Maud's face crinkled, and she blew her nose again.

Lady Petrie hovered nearby, her hands fluttering. Flora wondered if Maud might speak a bit more freely if her mother wasn't listening to every syllable.

"I do think poor Miss Petrie looks as if she could use some sustenance," Flora suggested, and waved at an untouched luncheon tray on a nearby table. "She is quite as pale as a spirit herself."

"I shall fetch some tea myself," Lady Petrie said quickly, and rushed out of the room in a cloud of rose perfume.

Flora took one of the silver brushes and a pink ribbon from the dressing table, and after helping Maud sit up began gently smoothing her tangled curls. She wasn't quite sure how to begin to demand a lady say if she'd been telling porkie pies. It wasn't like being backstage at the Follies, where a girl could just demand *"Oy, Molly, what's up with your fella then? Gone off him, 'ave ya?"* A girl like Maud Petrie, delicately well-bred, sheltered, bearing all her family's social hopes on her shoulders needed a bit more—grace. And Flora always found it so soothing herself when Mary brushed her hair.

She tied a neat bow with the ribbon and smoothed the wrinkles over the shoulders of Maud's pink velvet dressing gown. Then she went to push open the windows to let in some fresh air, or what little there could be had in London, to banish the scent of stale perfume and uneaten food. She noticed a large bouquet on the bedside table, pink and white roses and carnations.

"Those are very pretty," Flora said. She sat down on the end of the chaise.

Maud shrugged, but at least she had stopped crying.

"From the duke?"

"Yes." Her shoulders slumped, and she gave a little nod. "He is always so—correct."

Flora gently touched the edge of velvety white petal. "Rather more than correct, perhaps?"

"Affectionate, you mean, Madame Flowerdew?"

Maud said with a rough laugh. Her hands twisted together in her lap. "He would not be unkind, of course. I can tell he isn't *that* sort of man. But he's barely said twenty words to me as he steers me around a ballroom floor or drives me in the park. I imagine he might have more to say to my father's bank manager."

Flora could see that Maud was trying hard to seem worldly, sophisticated, but her eyes were bright with that fear. With the sense that her world was spinning away beneath her, and she could hardly cling on with her fingertips. The duke was a handsome prize indeed, one her friends would envy, her parents would kill to obtain for her—and for themselves. But if she loved someone else...

To her surprise, Flora found that her heart ached for Maud Petrie, for the pampered young lady who so easily possessed all Flora had been denied in her youth. Money, family, support, chances. But Maud seemed so lost and lonely right now. And she had looked so happy at the circus. If she had no wish to marry the duke, no one would listen to her, help her. Would she be desperate enough to dupe a superstitious father with ghostly curses?

And how would she do it?

Flora gently touched Maud's hand. It was icy cold. "It is true that marriages between titles and fortunes have an aspect of business about them. It must; your secure future depends on it. But what I've seen of Everton, he is no bounder. There could be fondness, partnership, even affection."

"I want more than that, though!" Maud burst out. "He's all right, that's true, and I want to please my parents, I really and truly do. I just—just..."

"You're in love with someone else," Flora said softly.

Maud burst into tears. "Oh, Madame Flowerdew! Of course *you* would know that, you can see so much. I

63

tried so, so hard not to, but he's just, oh! He is wonderful."

And clearly someone her parents would thoroughly disapprove of, Flora was sure. "Have you known him very long?"

"Forever!" Maud said, her face glowing suddenly like a summer's day. "He was my grandfather's last curate, and now the living is his. He came to London to meet with the bishop last month, and dined with us. He is ever so wonderful, so kind and funny and dear. And the vicarage is enormous, it would make a lovely home for us, and I could help him with his work. I would be an awful duchess, just awful. But I can't end up like my aunt Priscilla! Living in this house forever. Once, when she was young, she traveled and had fun, but no more. Now she is stuck here. I will be, too, if I can't marry Charles."

She burst into tears again, and collapsed over Flora's lap. Flora winced about the salty stains sure to set in her gray bombazine skirt, and smoothed Maud's hair again. "It is quite all right, my dear. I am sure your parents would understand if you spoke to them honestly. If you admitted what happened at the séance, too."

Maud sat straight up, her doe-like eyes blazing. "What happened? I had nothing to do with any of that!"

Flora was confused—and rather irked to have her easy solution snatched away. "You were not the ghost?"

Maud huffed indignantly. "Certainly not! How would I even do that? I was rather terrified by it all. But I admit I was also glad. How can I marry the duke if his family doesn't approve? Even if they're dead." She slid a crumpled photograph out from under a satin cushion and showed it to Flora. It was the bespectacled young man from the circus, his pale hair combed and shiny with pomade, a shy smile on his face. "This is my

Charles. How could I ever look into those perfect eyes and say I lied so hideously? I wouldn't do it."

Flora saw she had a point. The young vicar did look rather like a nativity play angel, and Maud seemed to be no schemer. Flora knew it took one to know one. But then who, or what, was the ghost? Sir Henry? Lady Petrie? That seemed rather silly. A duke as a son-in-law would get them ahead a lot faster than a vicar. Had Sir Henry known the old duke before, maybe had business dealings with him of some sort?

"Don't worry right now, Miss Petrie," she whispered. "I will find a way to help you tell your parents about your vicar, I promise." Being a romantic young couple's fairy godmother might even be fun. And she knew what it felt like to be pushed into a life that didn't feel like her own. But then what would she tell Benedict? He needed the Petrie money so much.

Lady Petrie returned with a large silver tea tray, looking determined to be cheerful as she laid out plates of cakes and sandwiches. "A charlotte russe, Maudie, your favorite!" She sliced at the cake, sending sugary scents into the freshened air.

Flora squeezed Maud's hand one more time, and Maud leaned closer with reluctant hope in her eyes. "You would help me, Madame Flowerdew, really?"

"Really. Now, my dear, you must eat something," Flora whispered back. "Being a vicar's wife requires robust health, don't you think? So many—parish duties and such." She really had no idea what a vicar's wife did, but she was sure it couldn't be much fun. Maud seemed to want it, though.

"Oh, yes, it does!' Maud dug happily into her cake, making her mother beam.

So—Lady Petrie and Maud probably weren't the ghost, nor was Mabel the Melodious. Or if she was, she was playing a long game indeed, sitting on a pile of priceless diamonds while laboring away in a circus wardrobe department.

But then who, oh *who*, could it be? Flora held back a sigh, and reached for a lemon tart on the tray. She hoped Benedict was having better luck with his old servants. And she felt a teeny twinge at having agreed to help his almost-fiancée marry someone else—but not too guilty-feeling after all.

~

When Flora emerged from Maud's chamber, she found Sir Henry himself in the foyer, leaving his top hat and gloves next to those enormous lilies on the pier table. He looked just as grumpy as he did during the séance, but she could see no way around him.

"Oh—erm. Good day, Madame Flowerdew," he said, rocking on his heels on the thick carpet, his hands behind him. "Very good of you to look in on my Maudie."

"Not at all, Sir Henry. It was a most unsettling experience for us all. I was most concerned about her." Flora tugged on her gloves as she made her way down the staircase.

"Yes, erm. You must have thought me rather a fool, a man of my worldly experience behaving thus."

Flora remembered his shouting, red-faced fury. "Certainly not. I was most upset myself. Such things do not occur often in my home, I assure you. Usually the spirits are most subdued. It is quite natural you would be concerned for your daughter."

"She's a good girl, is our Maudie. Naturally I want the best match possible for her, my only child. She can't end up a spinster, like my sister. My adopted sister, I should say, but she has always been here, part of the wallpaper. That would never do for my Maudie." He reached out and tapped his hand impatiently on the marble table, making the flowers tremble. "I suppose, er, the duke must have heard something of the fracas by now?"

Flora glanced down demurely, pretending to study the dark red and gold carpet. It was quite a nice rug indeed, eighteenth century maybe. "I fear something of the sort, yes."

Sir Henry scowled. "A family like that—well, I shall have to find a way to make it right again."

"I wondered if perhaps you would have doubts about the match now yourself, Sir Henry?"

His face reddened. "Well. Hmm. I may have, in the heat of the moment and all that. I've always had a bit of a temper, Madame Flowerdew, I admit it, and naturally I want my potential in-laws to approve of this marriage. Curses aren't what a man wants for his daughter on her wedding day."

"Indeed not."

"But then, the old cove *is* dead, no matter what. And Maudie couldn't hope for a better match than young Everton. I'd be a poor father indeed if I denied her the chance for a husband like that, such a fine chap."

A *fine chap* who came with a shining coronet of strawberry leaves—extra shine paid for by Sir Henry. "I am sure the duke would not let such things stand in the way of future happiness."

"No one should. Marital harmony is a great gift, an example I hope Lady Petrie and myself have shown Maud every day."

Flora nearly snorted, and covered it with a little cough. "I am sure your daughter derives great benefit from such an example."

"We have had our share of happiness, yes. And our Maudie has a chance to be a duchess now. Maybe even Mistress of the Robes one day! My grandson a duke..." His face turn on a dreamy cast, much like the one his daughter wore when she talked about her vicar.

Flora nodded, and briskly lowered the veil of her hat, and shook out her parasol. "A happy marriage is a blessing." Not one *she* would ever have, but maybe Maud Petrie would have a chance. Benedict, too, could find someone else, if his grandfather would just go away.

Sir Henry glanced at the stairs. "Erm, how is Maudie, then?"

"Upset, naturally, but resting now. Your wife took her a tray, and she is eating a bit. She will need her strength now, I fear."

"You are very sensible, Madame Flowerdew," Sir Henry said. "Do you have any suggestions as to how to persuade His Grace that we are assuredly respectable people? A suitable alliance?"

Flora rather imagined the state of the duke's roof at Thornhill Abbey would have made it a very suitable match. "Sir Henry, I would advise this. Perhaps with the help of another medium, I would like to hold another séance."

"Another séance?" he said doubtfully.

"To obtain more information. You did seem interested in the possibility. Perhaps then all parties would be reassured."

"Reassured. Yes. Perhaps you are correct, Madame Flowerdew." None of them mentioned what might happen if no more information was forthcoming. Or if the late duke made a mess of her chamber again.

"Have Lady Petrie write to me about which evening next week would suit, and I shall make the arrangements," she said, smoothing her gloves.

"Thank you, madame, you have been a great help." He handed her a small wallet. "Ah—what I owe, I believe, according to your invoice? There shall be that much again after our next meeting, and a great deal more when matters come to a satisfactory conclusion for my Maudie."

A satisfactory conclusion. Flora had no doubt what

he meant by that—walking his orange flower-bedecked daughter down the aisle of St. Margaret's, Westminster, to hand her over to the duke. But to Maud, it would mean a much simpler altar indeed. And to the duke...

Who knew what Benedict wanted, really? Her carefully honed intuition just seemed to fly away with him; she couldn't read him well at all. She tucked the wallet away into her reticule. No matter what happened, she did have to pay the coal merchant, after all. But the money didn't give her quite the glow of satisfaction it usually did.

Sir Henry hurried away, no doubt on some very important matter of business, and the butler opened the door for Flora.

"Madame Flowerdew," a woman called. "I am sure you must be a terrible busy woman, but if I may have just a moment?"

Flora turned to see Priscilla Petrie standing in the foyer. She had been quiet, unobtrusive, at the séance, but Flora saw now she was prettier than she seemed then, tall and slim with delicate features, dark eyes beneath arched brows, silver-streaked hair twisted into a simple knot atop her head, her plain chocolate-brown dress melting into the shadows. She smiled faintly and held out her hand.

"Of course," Flora said.

"How is Maud today? I have been so worried about her. To be disappointed in that way..."

"Have you?" Flora had not thought before that Miss Petrie was much concerned with her niece. She didn't seem much concerned about anything.

"Certainly. She is not like the rest of us, you see. She is quite—sensitive." Miss Petrie stepped closer, a quick, graceful, silent glide. "She deserves to be happy. Some of us—well, some of were never granted such a blessing. I should hate for that to befall Maudie."

Flora nodded, wondering if she had indeed misjudged Miss Petrie. "She is doing better for the moment, I think. She is taking some tea."

"Good. Thank you for all your help, Madame Flowerdew. I was thinking perhaps I would take her shopping, or to a tea shop she especially likes, something to take her mind off things." Miss Petrie glanced around the overstuffed foyer. "Get her out of this ghastly place for a time."

"I think that would be a very good idea, Miss Petrie."

Priscilla nodded, and hesitated for a moment before she said, "Do you really think it was the duke who spoke to us? Who can see things? *Know* things?"

"I have no idea," Flora answered honestly.

Miss Petrie nodded again, obviously distracted, and rushed away in a rustle of taffeta without another word. Flora was terribly glad to step out the door into the sunshine, away from that most peculiar family.

～

It was Mary's evening off at the flat, but she had left a tray of sandwiches and a bottle of cider for Flora's supper, and Evie had sent over a new folder of newspaper clippings. After Flora bathed and ate, she wrapped up in her dressing gown and settled down by the fire with Chou-Chou to sip her cider and read yet another pile of yellowed articles.

But they proved to be interesting indeed. The old duke and his wife (a daughter of a marquess, naturally, and considered the most beautiful deb of her Season) had a rather lively social life for a long time. They had been quite the force at Court and Society, and the duke a vociferous voice in the House of Lords. They made lots of enemies, and lots of friends who were probably secretly enemies, leaving lots of broken dreams in their sparkling wake.

And then they were sent off to India, where they lived grander than the viceroy himself. There were many drawings and accounts of balls, hunts, polo matches. Then the duchess began appearing in the diamonds, even at the polo. Flora could find very little about the stones themselves, beyond old legends of maharajahs.

The duke's only son, though, was indeed a very different sort from his parents, almost from the start. Wild, rackety, a habitue of the track and bawdy drinking clubs. Later on he became known as an explorer, his exploits followed in the press. Handsome, too, Flora thought as she studied an image of him. Rather like his own son, tawny-haired, Viking-strong. One photograph of him in Egypt showed him standing near the pyramids, a woman at his side, swathed in a pith helmet and veil, tall and strong.

In the next issue, he was back in England, marrying the daughter of a marquess. She was a pretty girl, but with a timid smile. And so very young. Flora shook her head, afraid she was looking at a mesalliance in the making.

Nine months after the wedding, that grand affair at St. Margaret's Sir Henry seemed to be dreaming of now, the wife had a baby son, Benedict, and the new husband and father was—gasp!--arrested as a public nuisance. His crime—throwing pamphlets about the abuses of the English in India at passersby in Hyde Park and then at the Foreign Office. Soon after, he vanished abroad for more of his adventuring. Flora wondered if the unwritten ending was stealing his mother's diamonds and then winding up dead in a Cornwall cave.

It was such a shocking, sordid tale, even to Flora's jaded eyes, that she could hardly believe it. She gulped down the last of her cider as she tried to organize what she knew—and what she didn't know, which was a great deal indeed.

Finally, her eyes crossing with it all, she pushed the

71

newspapers aside and reached for the afternoon post. Cheques for work finished, letters begging for appointments, that coal bill—and a note from Benedict, saying they were established for dinner with his great-uncle on the next night. The uncle who had been displaced for a dukedom by that wild, pamphlet-tossing young man, Benedict's father.

Well, she thought, even if she never did unravel this very tangled skein, she would at least get to spend a little more time with a duke...

Seven

You *really* could tell a lot about people from their houses, Flora thought as she left her wrap with Lord Edward's butler. The duke's grand mansion that didn't seem to belong to him at all; the Petries' halls stuffed with all the things they *thought* they should have. The townhouse of Benedict's great-uncle, brother to the overbearing ghost-duke, was quite different. Morris-designed wallpapers, green and blue with splashes of red poppies, and medieval-style tapestry cushions on the wooden chairs, blue glass vases on the tables, random paintings of fields and flowers and milkmaids, gave it all a cozy, bohemian feeling Flora quite enjoyed.

Benedict had mentioned that his uncle had possibly been unhappy about the old duke having a son and thus doing him out of the title, but Flora wondered if that was true. Everyone might *like* to be a duke, of course, but Lord Edward seemed to have settled into this life well enough. The house had the feeling of long contentment about it.

"Who am I, again?" she whispered to Benedict, as she took his arm and they followed the butler up the stairs. She glimpsed more floral paintings on the walls, pretty scenes of villages, and one portrait, a gentle-looking, auburn-haired lady dressed in an Aesthetic-style gown of peacock silk.

"A poor cousin on my mother's side, come to see the sites of London from your wee cottage in deepest Devon," Benedict whispered back. "I am giving you the treat of an evening dining out."

"You're not so bad at spinning a character, are you?" Flora said. She checked to make sure her hair was still firmly pinned in its plain twist, and smoothed the elbow-length sleeves of her dove gray dinner gown. It was a good thing she had Mary lay out the simple frock after all. "You should write for the stage!"

He looked quite pleased. "I might have to, if we can't find those diamonds and Miss Petrie refuses me," he said as the butler opened a door at the top of the stairs and ushered them into a drawing room.

Flora glanced back at the portrait of the lady with the kind eyes, as if for some reassurance, and followed Benedict inside.

"His Grace the Duke of Everton," the butler announced. "And Miss—Miss..."

"Miss—Fane," Benedict quickly supplied. He really should go in for the stage, Flora thought; Fane did sound like a good "poor relation" name.

The man who hurried forward had a wide, welcoming smile beneath a swooping, impressive mustache, and though rather portly had a look of Benedict about him. Flora noticed a younger man and a lady, both of them quite thin and worried-looking, on a settee by the fire. The room, just like the hall downstairs, was cozy and well lived-in, all blues and greens and artistic lines. She would have to find out who their decorator was.

"Benedict, my dear boy, how very grand to see you again," Lord Edward said, pumping Benedict's hand with that smile growing on his face. If he was resentful and angry, he was a good actor indeed, for he radiated nothing but delight and welcome. "I can't tell you how happy we were to receive your note, it has been much too long." He turned that smile onto Flora. "And Miss Fane. A cousin of poor Isabel's, yes? You are also most welcome, most welcome indeed."

"It was kind of you to invite me, Lord Edward," Flora said, trying to sound suitably meek and timid. She was seeing the great city from the silent depths of— Kent, was it? No, Devon.

"Not at all, the more the merrier, what? I am too solitary since my retirement from business," he said. Flora remembered he had worked at something in the City, most unusual for a duke's brother. "I see you were admiring the portrait of my dear Ellen, rest her soul. By Burne-Jones. She was so admired."

"She was very lovely," Flora said, and thought his taste in art was rather unusual for a duke's brother, as well. She couldn't imagine the late duke going in for the PRB.

"And as kind as she was beautiful," Lord Edward said, with a sad little shake of his head. "She was so fond of your father, Benedict, we both were. What a dear lad he was!"

"Was he, uncle?" Benedict said, sounding wistful and rather eager. "I fear I barely remember him at all. My grandfather always said he was a wild n'er-do-well."

Lord Edward pursed his lips. "Well, he *would* say that, wouldn't he? My brother thought everyone had to be only one way—and know their place. I fear I never did. Nor did your father."

"I should certainly like to know more about him," Benedict said.

"And I am very happy to tell you everything I re-member! But now let me introduce you to my son, Lawrence, and his wife Regina."

Flora surreptitiously studied the lady for any hint of

diamonds, but she wore only pearls, and a few paste buttons on her oyster-colored gown. She held out her hand, adorned with just a gold band, and said, "You are very welcome, Miss Fane. I am quite glad to have another lady to talk to for once! Do sit next to me."

Lawrence didn't look so welcoming. "Yes. Indeed. Let me pour you some sherry."

As he went to the sideboard, Flora sat down in his abandoned spot and watched as Lord Edward and Benedict took chairs across from them.

"Tell me, Benedict, how do you find Thornhill Abbey and Everton House?" Lord Edward asked, taking a glass of amber liquid from his son. "Very much different from when you last saw them? Surely it has been some time."

Flora took a sip of the sweet sherry, and realized she actually didn't know *where* Benedict had been before appearing in London to get engaged to Miss Petrie. She actually didn't know a great deal about him at all, which was an odd realization, since she felt as if she'd known him for ages. Very strange.

"Not at all. In fact, everything is exactly the same. It's quite eerie, really. Frozen."

Lord Edward nodded. "Just like when I was a child. You must make changes, my dear boy. Shake things up there, as your father would have done if he had lived. Change was not my brother's forte. Not at all."

"Yet he does seem to have traveled a bit," Benedict said. "My grandfather, that is. To India."

"For the service of the Crown and the glory of the Everton title," Lawrence said in a sardonic tone, raising his sherry glass.

Lord Edward laughed. "True, true. He did not travel as your father did, Benedict. His kind heart saw the world in a very different light from my brother."

"I have been reading about his adventures," Regina

said. "So dashing! And those ever so romantic rumors…"

"Romantic rumors?" Flora said, more eagerly than she intended. She tried to look demurely down into her glass.

"How rackety you must think us all, Miss Fane," Lord Edward said. "Isabel's family was much quieter, I remember, much involved in their country pursuits. She herself was such a shy little thing, though very pretty, of course. Perhaps that was what happened."

"What *did* happen?" Benedict asked.

"Oh, it was in—Egypt, I think. Or maybe Persia!" Regina said. Flora hoped she got to sit next to her at dinner. She definitely seemed like the gossipy one of the little group. Lawrence was quietly draining his glass, as if not paying attention to them much at all. Or maybe he, and not his father, was the one who was resentful? "They say he fell in love with a beautiful young lady, an explorer like himself, but it simply could not be. I sometimes wish I could have traveled like that! How fortunate your father was, Benedict. Even if there was heartbreak…"

Much to Flora's disappointment, the butler appeared again to announce dinner was served. Lord Edward offered Flora his arm and led her toward the dining room, with Regina and Lawrence behind them and Benedict trailing, falling a bit behind to study an array of silver-framed photographs on a table.

"I'm sorry we are so informal this evening, Miss Fane," Lord Edward said. "We don't usually entertain in grand style, anyway, and we wanted Benedict to have a real *en famille* dinner."

"I am sure he much appreciates it, Lord Edward," she answered. "From what I have heard, family events have been quite a rarity for the duke."

He sadly shook his head. "So true, my dear, so true.

Grand events were *all* my brother and his wife knew how to do, and Isabel was always so delicate. My wife and I would have enjoyed seeing much more of Benedict and his father, but it was—well, difficult."

"Families can be such odd things indeed. My own life is very quiet, but I am so interested in how others live their time." That was true enough. Her life was not exactly *quiet*, not with ghosts plaguing her flat, but it could be lonely. She often existed in the stories of others. And the ducal family seemed odd indeed. "How exciting a life of exploration must be! Or a career in the City, as you have done."

He laughed. "It had its moments, yes. Very different from how I grew up. But I am quite enjoying my retired days."

He led her into the dining room, an oval space with walls painted a light, glowing blue and cream, a fire cheerfully crackling in a white marble grate, dancing over the silver and delicate, flower-painted china on a small, round table. Flora was indeed seated very near Regina, which hopefully promised more information on the "romantic rumors."

As the soup was served, and the gentlemen talked on Lawrence's work at an import company, Flora leaned closer to Regina and said quietly, "Did the duke's father really have a romance in Egypt? It sounds like a novel! Kisses by moonlight near the pyramids."

Regina's eyes sparkled. "Oh, it does! Like *Passion on the Nile*. Have you read that one? It is a great favorite of mine."

"Indeed I have!" Flora was rather delighted to have found a sister devotee of the penny dreadfuls. "The one where there is a murder on the boat, and a pharaoh's ghost that wanders the riverbanks. I thought I would scream aloud."

"I fear I did! I quite alarmed Lawrence, but he is accustomed to my ways by now. We were not blessed with children, so reading has always been my great consolation." She rang a small bell by her plate and the fish course was brought in. Despite her seeming flightiness, Regina seemed to have the household well under control. Maybe she was good at other deceptions, too. "To have had a life of real adventure, though—how splendid it must be."

"And to have a heartbreaking romance, as the duke's father did?"

Regina sighed. "I do wish I knew more about it all. It was never spoken of, you see, especially after the poor man died so horribly in Cornwall. And Isabel in such frail health! One could not disturb her."

"What are you whispering about so intently?" Lawrence suddenly demanded, tapping his wine glass for a refill.

Regina giggled nervously. "Oh, books, of course! You know me, darling. Miss Fane is another great reader."

Lawrence rolled his eyes. "Heaven help us."

Flora turned to Lord Edward. "You mentioned your life now is very different from your childhood at Thornhill Abbey, Lord Edward. I do enjoy visiting great houses when their gardens are open, and have always been curious about what it's like to live in such a place."

Lord Edward smiled ruefully. "Believe me, my dear Miss Fane, it is much more enjoyable to visit than to live there. Great, cold, empty places they can be. Frozen in aspic."

"But it might be rather fun to try it," Regina said wistfully.

"We shall never know, shall we," her husband muttered.

"You are all very welcome at Thornhill at any time," Benedict said. "I have a sense I will be quite lonely there."

"But are you not be married soon?" Regina asked.

"We have heard you've been seen at the theater and driving in the park with a certain young lady!"

A dull flush touched Benedict's cheekbones. "That remains to be seen. I shall have to marry soon, I know, but family will always be welcome at my houses. I especially need much advice on refurbishment! Your wallpapers here are so beautiful, uncle, you must inform me where I can acquire them. I know nothing about such things, and have so much to learn."

Flora laughed to think how she had never talked more about warehouses in her life than she had the last few days, but she had to confess she would like those wallpapers for herself. It was rather fun to talk about household arrangements and fashion with a lady.

After half an hour of trying to include Lawrence in conversation beyond "terribly foggy lately, yes" (really, he was one of most annoyingly taciturn people Flora had ever met; usually men were all too eager to regale a girl about everything concerning themselves), she excused herself to "mend her hem." She was directed to Regina's dressing room at the end of the corridor, and took her time to examine what she could of the house.

It all seemed as if Lord Edward was exactly what he said—a businessman who prospered and was content not to be a duke. Everything about the pretty furniture, the slightly shabby carpets, the photographs and paintings, whispered of a settled-in life. Except one chamber. When Flora peeked into what seemed to be a library, dimly illuminated by one lamp, she saw a large silk banner embroidered with the Everton crest hanging from the ceiling. Perhaps the old duke wasn't quite the only one to take pride in the title.

She examined the array of leather-bound books on the shelves, all of them stamped in gold with more of that crest. She slipped a few off to flip through the pages, and found one that seemed to be underlined and had notes in the margins in the old duke's crabbed handwriting. She slipped it into her handbag, glad she had brought one large enough to hold a spinster's knitting, and rearranged the shelf to look undisturbed.

As she tiptoed into the corridor and closed the door behind her, she heard hissing whispers coming from behind a tall, marble plant stand, and she stayed in the shadows, straining to listen.

It was Lawrence and Regina.

"...told you never to gossip so! Especially with people we do not know," Lawrence said.

"Surely you could not have meant with family! It is not gossiping then, merely conversation, and I do not gossip anyway," Regina hissed back.

"The duke is a stranger to us, and his cousin even more so. We don't need to discuss any family peccadilloes with them. How often must I tell you? My cousin's romance was long ago, and can have no good reflection on us. We have our business reputation to consider. Now, come along. No more chatter."

Flora tiptoed toward the drawing room. Perhaps this wasn't such a contented house after all. She really needed to discover more about Benedict's father's romantic life. Encouraging Regina's "gossipy" ways wasn't so difficult. She should invite the lady to a tea shop sometime, where her husband couldn't overhear.

"Ah, there you are, Miss Fane," Lord Edward said as she took her seat again. "My son has just gone to send for more coffee. I was telling Benedict about the folly that used to be in the garden at Thornhill, if he should want to restore it..."

~

Flora stared out the carriage window as they jolted through the London streets. Evening fog had started to roll in, casting the darkness as something silvery and shivery. Through the haze, she glimpsed chimneys and glowing windows, figures slipping past like ghosts. Indeed, she hoped they were *not* ghosts, she'd had quite enough of that sort of thing for the moment.

It was very different from the view through the grimy windows of a hansom or tram. She wrapped her cloak tighter around her shoulders, and leaned back against the plush velvet seats as she tucked her feet closer to the warmer on the carpeted floor. She could get used to all that! Velvet seats, warm toes, whisked from place to place in minutes, helped in and out by footmen.

But she knew too well she better *not* get used to it. This would all end when they found the diamonds and Benedict married poor Miss Petrie, her vicar-love notwithstanding.

Benedict, from his seat across from hers, also stared out the window, his forehead crinkled as if he was deep in thought. It was really too adorable, and Flora had to tuck her hands into the folds of her cloak to keep from smoothing out those lines.

"Your relatives seem quite nice," she said. Except for whispering behind plants, that was.

"Yes, very kind indeed. I should have kept in better communication with them over the years."

"Your uncle does appear to have missed you," she said. She took a deep breath and plunged on, "Where have you been all this time?"

He turned to her with a startled glance. "Where have I been?"

"Yes. While you were away from your family, before becoming the duke. You must have been very busy."

"So I was." He looked back out the window, the silence stretching across the carriage for a long moment. "I thought I might try to follow in my father's footsteps, travel a bit, that sort of thing. See what was so much more exciting to him than England. Than his family."

Flora remembered the photograph of Benedict's father in Egypt with those ladies, and Regina's tales of romance. Maybe Benedict had followed in those foot-steps? "And was it? Exciting?"

He laughed. "Not very. Oh, it was interesting, of course, and I saw some beautiful places. Florence, Athens, Turkey. But I didn't find anything—well, anything really *different*, if you see what I mean."

Flora nodded. "I think so. People are people wherever you go."

"Exactly. Happy, sad, angry, deceitful, helpful, destructive. All sorts. Just with different trees and mountains. It had its own satisfactions, though, even some petty ones like receiving my grandfather's angry letters. Those were entertaining."

She smiled to think of. She could just imagine. "You weren't being a proper duke-in-waiting, were you?"

"Not in the slightest. No sense of duty, you see, just like my father. I should have made things even more satisfying, presented him with an American duchess after I visited California."

"Oh, I don't know," Flora said, pushing down an annoying pang at the thought of his imagined American wife. "Lots of gents here are marrying Americans lately. They say even the Duke of Marlborough has his eye on one."

"But they are heiresses all. I would have found myself some cowgirl. Or maybe a Harvey Girl!"

"What's a Harvey Girl?"

"A cafe waitress of sorts, but they only take the cream of their applicants. Pretty, smart, efficient girls who are paid very well to work in hotels across the American West."

"Larks, but I should get one of those jobs! But she sounds too respectable to present to your grandfather. Maybe you do need an Annie Oakley sort. I saw her at a show once, at the Lyceum Theater. All leather skirts and feathers, and an enormous hat! She could split a playing card edge-on at thirty paces, astonishing."

"Hmm, no, it sounds like my grandfather would have found her much too useful in shooting season to really disapprove," Benedict laughed. "Better to do what I did, I suppose, and not provide them with a duchess at all. I never met a lady who deserved such a sad fate as living with my grandparents, anyway."

Flora didn't think being married to Benedict would be such a "sad fate" at all. He was so handsome, so interesting, and seemed so kind. And with a big house and diamonds as the cherry on top...

She glanced at him sharply, suddenly wondering in a flash of thought if *he* possibly could have hidden the diamonds himself, as a way to make his grandfather angry. It didn't seem possible, really, but then—people *were* people, and did some awfully peculiar things sometimes. And there were no diamonds on offer to Maud Petrie now, which was what brought them all here in the first place.

Flora reminded herself sternly that she was just doing a job, and she turned to look back out the window. They were close to her flat now, rolling past the small park at the end of the lane. "Your uncle didn't really seem peeved to be done out of the title. He seems happy enough with his life, and I don't get the sense that he's shamming."

Benedict gave her an admiring glance, or one she *hoped* was admiring and not incredulous at her naivety concerning Lord Edward. "You do have a sense of people, don't you, Flora? You *see* them."

She shrugged. "Women's intuition. And it's my job. Helping people find what they're really looking for." She wished she could read *him* better. "Some people are more elusive than others. And some are better at deceit, of course."

"My uncle has had years to come to terms with not being a duke. He defied the Everton name, too, by making a fine career for himself. But what about his son?"

Flora thought of Lawrence berating his wife behind the plant stand. "Harder to read, I think. The quiet ones often are. He seems a bit dour."

"His wife isn't very quiet."

"No, she is very friendly indeed. I don't think her husband cares for that much, though. Not at all. I wonder if her talkative ways have landed them in some trouble before." She tucked her cloak closer around her. "Do you know anything about that gossip concerning your father and his love for a lady not your mother?"

Benedict frowned. "I—no, I don't think so. I suppose I would assume he had affairs and such in his travels, but one doesn't like to speculate on parents that way."

Flora thought of her own parents, her unknown father and her mother who hadn't scruple to let everyone "think of her that way." She wished she'd been able not to know, before she was sent off to the orphanage. "Hmm, yes."

"Why? Was that what you and Regina were whispering about?"

"Oh, nothing certain, just gossip she'd heard. I thought it was interesting, that's all."

"Who was she, then? This love of my father's?"

Flora shrugged. "I have no idea. Maybe it's somewhere in all those letters we haven't read yet."

The carriage rolled to a stop at the front steps of Flora's building, and she gathered up her handbag, heavy with the purloined book. "Thank you for a most interesting evening, Your G—Benedict."

As the footman opened the carriage door and let down the steps, Benedict briefly touched her gloved hand, his fingers warm and tingly. His face was in the shadows, and she couldn't tell if he felt it, too, that strange little jolt. "Shall we go over more of the letters tomorrow, Flora?"

"I have an appointment with a Madame Flowerdew client. Looking for her lost cat, the poor thing. But I will send a message."

"Of course. Thank you for going with me this evening. I'm afraid it must have been dull for you."

Flora let herself drift her fingertips over his cheek, and smiled. "Believe me, dukie, nothing about all of this is dull. Good night."

She hurried into the house, not looking back, and let herself into the flat. Mary had already gone to bed, so it was all dark and quiet, just one lamp burning on Flora's dressing table. The sheets were turned back, her nightgown laid out, a cup of cocoa on the bedside table, and Chou-Chou snoring on a nest of pillows. A note on her bedside table said that the Petries agreed to the rescheduled séance, and now she just had to invite Benedict.

Flora was able to change out of the simple gray dress herself, and she sat down with a sigh in front of the mirror to let her hair down. It was true, it hadn't been a dull evening at all. Families were never dull to her, since she had never been in the middle of one herself, and a family of ducal caliber seemed even more mysterious. Only really they were quite like anyone else she might meet, underneath. And she was intrigued to think Benedict's father could have had a doomed romance. If she could only find out more...

She shook her head and reached for her cocoa. Every step forward in this matter just seemed to propel her back three, show her how much she didn't know at all!

Chou-Chou suddenly let out a growl, low and rough. Startled, Flora glanced over at the dog, who was standing on her pillows, her fluffy ruff of amber fur standing on edge.

Flora frowned. Everything was just as quiet as when

she had first opened the flat door. What could be upsetting Chou-Chou? Yet those growls grew deeper, louder, as if they emanated from a much larger dog. "Chou-Chou, lambikins, what is it? What..."

A bright flash exploded in the mirror, and Flora ducked, sure she would be struck with flying glass. Nothing broke, but more flashes followed, gold, green, turquoise-blue, like a Bonfire Night fireworks show.

Her brain humming with panic, blood fizzing through her veins, she crawled across the floor to wrap her arms tightly around Chou-Chou, who was shivering and barking frantically. She raised one doggie paw and pointed toward the mirror.

"Where are my diamonds?" a roar went around the room, seeming to whip up a whirlwind that tore at her curtains and tossed the pictures on the walls. "I came to you for help, girl—*me*, who never asks for help! And there is nothing. What have you and my worthless grandson been doing?"

Flora bristled at Benedict being called "worthless." She sat up and stared into the misty mirror. "Quite a lot, actually, you old ingrate! I've taken time out of my own work to run around Town doing *your* business. Mabel, your brother..."

"They are just as useless as Benedict! Just give my brother a good kick and he'll tell you any secret, no backbone at all. As for Mabel..."

"Yes! What about Mabel?" Flora shouted. Chou-Chou barked in agreement. "You treated her horribly! Leaving her to sew her fingers to the bone in a circus costume closet. After she put up with your nonsense for so long."

The howling wind subsided just a titch. "Yes—well. It wasn't meant to be that way. It's hardly my fault she didn't secure her investments."

"As if you left her any investments. And what about your wife?"

"Haven't you talked to Harriet yet? Do I have to tell you how to do everything?"

"France is a long way away, and some of us can't just jaunt off on a second's notice. Some of us have to work for our bread!"

A bolt of bright-white light shot out from the mirror, and Flora clutched tighter at Chou-Chou. "Speaking of which," she went on, hoping her voice didn't shake, "I'm having another séance with your grandson and the Petries tomorrow. If you want to be helpful at all, you'll show up. You're the one who wants these diamonds so much."

The wind picked up, faster and faster, colder. Flora shivered, and even Chou-Chou ducked under the bedclothes. "My grandson can't marry without those diamonds! He will destroy the Everton line. Find them, now!"

"The séance..."

"Well. I'll try. Tomorrow is my whist night with Prince Albert and Charlemagne," came the gruff reply. Chou-Chou peeked out of the sheets, and immediately started to levitate from the bed. Furious, Flora caught the dog and held her tight.

"Stop it right now, you horrible old man, or I won't help you any longer," she shouted, and the wind abruptly died. The lights were gone, and the room was in dim light again. Even the pictures were straight on the walls.

Flora ran to look out the window and behind her dressing table, wondering if someone was playing a horrible joke on her. Nothing was there, though. She dashed back to the bed and jumped under the blankets, clutching at her shivering dog. She had just about had enough with that ghost, with diamonds, and with playing theater games with duke's brothers and mistresses and the Petries. They upset Chou-Chou, wrecked her furniture, and took up her time.

But there *was* Benedict, and his lovely blue eyes and crooked smile. And the circus had been rather fun. Also, the fact that there was whist in the after-life was an odd comfort. She wondered if Prince Albert was any good at it.

"Oh, Chou-Chou, my poor lambikins," she whispered to her now-calmer dog. "Whatever is going to happen next?"

Eight

"Will you all take your places in the circle, please?" Flora said in her low, soft "Madame Flowerdew" voice. She glanced quickly around the small séance circle to be sure all was at rights.

Of course it was; Mary was the essence of efficiency. The rounded walls were hung with lengths of black and purple cloth, holding out light and muffling noise from the street and the other flats. The oval table was also draped in purple, with a circle of candles atop the amethyst damask the only light aside from a lamp in the corner. A shallow glass bowl filled with water, and a silver-edged mirror on a stand were the only other table adornments. Except for Chou-Chou, who sat beside the bowl calmly cleaning her paws. As if butter wouldn't melt and she hadn't been terrified of ghosts last night, the little fraudster.

Flora shivered a bit as she remembered the phantom shouts, the wind whistling around her bedroom. She didn't mind admitting she'd been a beastly coward, too. That horrid old duke taking over her house! It had to stop.

She took a deep breath, and the floral-patterned lace veil of her hat fluttered. Tonight's event required a step up in the Madame disguise. In addition to her usual purple satin gown, heavily crusted with jet embroidery and a black velvet capelet, topped with her curled black wig, she wore a pair of blue-tinted glasses and a black tricorne hat with the long veil. Mary had carefully powdered Flora's face snow-white and rouged her lips to the hue of port wine. Black satin gloves covered her hands.

Feeling quite armored-up, she took her seat and gestured to her guests to gather around. Evie looked avidly delighted, as if settling in for a particularly lurid grand guignol performance yet sensibly ready for anything in a walking suit of Harris tweed and felt hat. Her hand kept inching toward her tapestry handbag, as if for her notepad and pencil, but journalist's notes were strictly forbidden in circle. Not that Flora worried about it; Evie had a memory like a steel trap, she wouldn't forget anything.

Next to her sat Benedict, a little, suspicious frown on his face. He whispered a word to Maud on his other side, and she gave him a watery smile. Her eyes were no longer reddened with weeping for her vicar, but she did look pale and listless, shivering a bit in her wispy pale pink chiffon and lace gown.

With Maud sat her aunt, Miss Priscilla Petrie, her face expressionless, her gaze far away, as if ghosts held no interest for her. Sir Henry and his wife seemed anxious, and Flora knew they sensed this evening's events might close the deal for their daughter's elevation to duchesshood.

Mary stood behind Flora, watchful in her plain black dress and white cap, careful to keep any shenanigans at bay. Flora worried, though, that if the old duke got up to his tricks, even Mary couldn't stop him.

Flora remembered the words of her old mentor, the Great Clairvoyant Medium Madame Buttercup. *"My dear,"* she would always say. *"If things seem to be getting out of hand, or if you have a doubting Thomas in your circle, immediately end it, break the circle of hands, extinguish the candles. Immediately!"*

Flora was quite sure none of that would work on the cranky ghost duke. But this was worth a try. Surely *someone* here knew more than they were saying about the diamonds.

She nodded to Mary, who put out the lamp in the corner, plunging them into a tiny, shadowed circle. Chou-Chou sat up straight, her caramel-colored eyes shining, tiny ears swiveling.

"Will you all join hands, please?" Flora said softly. She felt Evie and Sir Henry take her gloved hands. Maud sniffled, the only sound in the room. Flora closed her eyes and tried to calm her mind, tried not to worry about what might happen next. To worry about if the duke showed up—or if he *didn't* show up.

"Our beloved ones," she chanted. "We bring you gifts from life unto death. Commune with us, move among us."

For several long moments there was only silence. Then Chou-Chou began growling, low and deep in her throat. When Flora peeked at her through the lace veil, she saw Chou-Chou's ruff of amber fur standing on end.

A breeze swept around the table, not cold and violent like last night, but warm, soft. It smelled of—was that jasmine? Jasmine and something like salty ocean breezes. A sugary cake.

Flora heard a gasp, yet she couldn't tell from where it came.

"Spirit, reveal yourself," she said. "You are most welcome here. Do you bring a message for one of us?"

Chou-Chou's growling grew deeper, the wind moving faster. Now it seemed to carry an essence of a desert with it, some sort of oasis of fruit and flowers, grittiness. Flora longed to toss back her suddenly too-heavy cape.

This was not the duke. Perhaps her skills as a medium were rather improving.

"What do you wish to tell us?" she cried.

Maud gasped. "Oh, look! Look!"

Everyone peered into the mirror where Maud stared. It had just reflected the dark walls, the flicker of the candles. Now there was a *face*. Pale and blurry, like a cloud, but assuredly a face. Lady Petrie cried out, and Flora almost screamed herself, but managed to bite her lip. Chou-Chou went down on her front paws and bared her teeth, yet she backed away from the glass.

"Who are you?" Flora whispered. "You are among friends here. If you mean us no harm..."

"Oh, how terribly exciting!" Evie murmured, squeezing Flora's hand.

No words came from the glass, but that scent of tropical flowers increased, almost too rich to breathe in.

"Don't let him find it," a low drift of a voice hissed, from nowhere and everywhere. "Never, never!"

"The diamonds, you mean?" Flora asked. "Who should not find them? Where are they?"

"Never, never." The face sharpened in the glass for only an instant, a woman, the pale skin, a sharp chin, dark hair.

"What..." Miss Petrie began, starting to stand up. "No."

"Miss Petrie, don't break the circle!" Flora cried. It was too late. The flowers were gone, the glass iced over, and a cold, howling wind broke out. The black and purple hangings dipped and swayed.

"*My* diamonds! Mine, I tell you," that familiar voice roared.

Flora held back a frustrated sigh. Just when she thought she was getting somewhere! That old duke really was a boor *and* a bore. No wonder no one had liked him in life. She was just surprised he could find whist partners now.

"If you want them back so much, then help us," Flora said. "Point us in a useful direction! And why do you want them so much anyway? The dead can't wear them."

"How do you know? None of you have been here." One of the candles blew out, the silver holder shaking so much she was sure it would tip over. "They are for her! The future duchess. To break the curse. I didn't believe before. Now we must."

Maud Petrie shrieked as she was hauled out of her chair, her arm seized by an invisible force. Benedict and Miss Priscilla Petrie grabbed for her, holding her down. It seemed even the circle wasn't needed by the ghosts any more.

"I don't want it, I don't want it," Maud sobbed. "I can't bear it! Oh, do let me go."

"You're the key, girl," the duke shouted, yet his voice was losing its forceful violence, as if he slipped back into the ether. "You hold the answer."

"I don't!" Maud shouted back. "I don't understand any of this."

Lady Petrie was crying hysterically, so much so that Mary leaped forward with the smelling salts she kept in her pocket. Evie reached for her notepad. It was definitely time to take Madame Buttercup's advice and try to break the circle, even if it was futile.

"Everyone, separate!" Flora demanded firmly. She ran around lighting all the lamps she could find. Chou-Chou hopped off the table and scurried away, the wee coward. Or maybe she was the wise one. "Spirits, be gone from this place! I command you."

Everyone looked startled in the sudden light. Miss Priscilla Petrie, her face chalky and eyes wide but steady and sensible, led Maud and her mother out of the room, handing them handkerchiefs and a flask. Miss Petrie glanced back for a moment, staring at the mirror, before she shook her head and left.

"Well," Sir Henry said, even his booming voice quiet now. "If my daughter's safety can't be guaranteed even in a ducal house..."

"I am sure it can," Flora told him. "We will have this sorted in no time at all, Sir Henry, I assure you."

"I don't know about all this," he muttered, and hurried after his family. Mary rushed after to find their cloaks. "It doesn't seem respectable."

When they were gone, the door shut behind them, the silence almost deafening it echoed so much, Flora wearily led Mary, Evie, and Benedict to the regular sitting room, and poured out snifters of her strongest brandy. She tossed aside her hat, veil, and wig with a relieved sigh, and plopped down on a chaise.

"Well," she said. "That was certainly a how d'ye do."

Evie pulled out her pencil and started scribbling madly. "Who was that in the glass? Certainly not the old duke."

"No." Flora frowned, trying to recall any fleeting detail. It had been a woman, but her features had been blurry. "I have no idea. Did you recognize her, Benedict?"

He shook his head, and took a long gulp of the brandy. He looked pensive, almost sad. Because he might be about to lose his fiancée? How was Maud "the key" to all of this? "Not at all. A lady, I think, with dark hair. And a white hat? Or was that mist?"

"Oh, yes," Flora said, remembering the swirl of white veil the figure seemed to wear. "Maud and her mother did seem very upset, poor things. I'm glad Miss Petrie stayed so calm to help them."

"Well, one doesn't like to be yanked out of one's chair by a ghost, I'm sure, but Maud Petrie does often seem watery-eyed to me," Evie muttered as she flipped back through the pages of her notepad. "Oh, I meant to tell you, Flora, I did a bit of a dig through the old news-

95

paper files and found a strange article about the duke's old butler."

Benedict glanced up sharply. "Talbot? I did have the thought we should find him and see what he remembers, he used to know everything that happened in my grandfather's house."

"I'm afraid I don't know where this Talbot might be, but his brother was someone who was, as they say, known to Scotland Yard."

"Indeed?" Benedict laughed. "I wish he'd come around Thornhill when I was a boy, it might have livened things up a bit."

"I daresay it would!" Evie said. "His name was Richard Talbot, and it seems he was often in trouble with gaming establishments around Town, not paying his debts, suspected of thievery and common assault."

"Was?" Flora asked, pouring out more brandy. Chou-Chou jumped up into her lap and yawned widely.

"It seems so. He disappeared after promising a certain Mrs. Milly, owner of a fine gentlemen's establishment in Soho, a diamond in exchange for his rather large debts."

"Always diamonds," Flora sighed. "Never thought I would say this, but I'm getting a bit tired of diamonds."

"Oh, but it was not just any diamond," Evie said. "He told her he could give her an *Everton* diamond, if she wouldn't set her bully-boys onto him."

Flora sat straight up. "He had one of the Everton diamonds? The butler's brother?"

"So he told Mrs. Milly. But he never showed up to make good his signed IOU. It seems she didn't just have gangs of bully-boys, but a friend at Scotland Yard, and she went to demand Dick Talbot be found and made to fulfill his debts. He never was found, though. Vanished."

"Fascinating," Flora said. "Where could he have gone?"

"No one knows, but pretty far I'd say, if he did have the jewels," Evie said. She glanced at Benedict. "Or it might be that Dick gave them to his brother, your butler? For safekeeping? Maybe the butler even took them in the first place."

Benedict shook his head thoughtfully. "I wouldn't have thought so back then. Talbot was with my grandfather for years, he started at Thornhill as a boot boy. He was very proper, very stiff-shouldered. He kept the household under strict control, it was why my grandfather liked him so much. He could be nice sometimes, though, and would give me barley twists."

"Do you know anything about his family?" Flora asked.

"Not a thing. I was just a boy, and rather intimidated by him. How funny he should have such a rogue brother."

"People are always odd," Flora said. "Is Talbot still alive? Would he talk to us?"

"I'll keep looking for him. There should be some records somewhere," Benedict said. "The estate still pays out a pension, so he must be alive. I confess I'm curious about him! What will we find next? That our housekeeper kept betting books for the Derby? The head footman was a safe-breaker?"

"Oh, Flora," Evie said merrily. "I am so glad we're friends! I haven't had so much fun in an age."

Nine

What a lot of dull books the Evertons had, Flora thought as she turned yet another moldy page. It told her nothing yet about diamonds or lost loves! Very disappointing.

There was a quick knock at the door, and Mary peeked in. Flora glanced up, relieved to be distracted from the book. "The duke is here!"

For an instant, Flora thought Mary meant the ghostly duke, and her shoulders stiffened. *Oh, not again!* They had just finished cleaning up after the chaotic scene, she didn't want to deal with him again yet. Then she remembered, it had to be Benedict. He said he would call that day and take her to see his old butler.

"Oh," she gasped, and tried to smooth her rumpled hair. Tried not to let those ridiculous excited butterflies flutter inside of her. There was not time to do more than put on the jacket of her blue walking suit and pin a hat to her hair, hoping she looked presentable.

"So you found the butler!" she said cheerfully as she met Benedict in the foyer. "That was fast."

He turned to her with a smile that set those wretched butterflies floating again. "It proved rather a simple thing, I just looked over the Everton financial books. I owe him a call anyway, and I admit I am very curious about what he has to say about his rascal brother."

"So am I. Imagine—a sibling who is a thief known to Scotland Yard! I had some shady relatives, but nothing so impressive."

"Really?" he said, his eyebrow raised in interest. "I should enjoy hearing those tales. You know all about my annoying relatives."

Flora doubted she knew *all* about his family, and she certainly didn't want him to know about hers. An unknown father, a mother who left her behind at an orphanage. What she *did* know about them was cheap and sordid, not worthy of a novel at all, unlike ghostly dukes. Benedict was so shiny-good, so handsome and dignified and kind, she couldn't bear to see his eyes dim when he looked at her, when he knew the whole truth about her life. She wouldn't have him in that life much longer anyway.

"Oh, they're very boring really," she said lightly, and turned away to tug on her gloves. "Very ordinary."

His carriage was waiting outside, glossy black in the pale sunshine, the gilded ducal crest gleaming. A small crowd of neighbors loitered nearby, trying not to seem to be gawking but clearly with no business nearby. It was a respectable, prosperous neighborhood, but not one much frequented by dukes. For the first time in this adventure, Flora worried a bit about her reputation. She had no desire to move.

She ducked her head under her hat, and let the footman help her up onto the velvet seats. Benedict sat down across from her and knocked on the door, setting them into motion.

"How was Miss Maud today?" Flora asked, fiddling with the button on her glove. "She seemed rather overset after the séance, though who could blame her."

Benedict stared out the window, expressionless. "She isn't receiving callers, so I had to send a note to her.

I feel terrible; if not for my family, she wouldn't be upset at all."

Flora wasn't so sure about that. Maud Petrie would still be in love with her vicar, and her parents would still want her to marry a duke. She wondered if Maud could really possibly have been clever enough to plan the whole ghostly thing to get out of the situation, but she didn't see how the girl could have gotten into Flora's own bedroom and scared Chou-Chou. "It was the Petries who came to me in the first place."

"Why *did* they come to you? Did they think talking to ghosts would ease any doubts about the marriage?"

Flora thought back, trying to remember how the Petries had come to be clients. It was all rather made hazy by the dramatic events since. "I think it was actually Miss Petrie, Sir Henry's sister, who first wrote to me. She said Maud was the Petries' only child and they wanted to be certain she would prosper in her new life. Perhaps Lady Petrie's parents had once been very interested in spiritualism? Though I shouldn't think so, she's a vicar's daughter."

"They seem a rather odd family, don't they?" Benedict laughed. "Not as odd as mine, of course."

"How did you meet Miss Maud?"

"At a dance, not long after I came to London. She seemed rather nice, shy. Different from the other ladies I met. They were all so very eager for a duke, not really for *me*. They didn't even seem to see me. Maud just—talked to me. I knew I needed to marry, and I wanted a wife with—well, with a spirit of kindredness, I suppose. Someone I could be friends with, unlike my grandparents who rarely spoke to each other at all unless it was about estate matters. Maud is a nice young lady, and her father did seem interested in the match. He also seemed interested in helping with the leaking roof at Thornhill, as terrible as that sounds."

They were both quiet for a long moment as they

watched the streets roll past the windows. "Perhaps," he finally said, "I mistook her reluctance for shyness. I can't marry her if that is the case, of course. But how can I persuade her to really confide in me? Especially if my grandfather has frightened her."

Flora shook her head, wishing *she* could confide in him. But Maud's secrets were Maud's to tell, and Flora would never betray another woman. Even for Benedict. "Maud is a lady of hidden depths. Once she has had time to rest and think, you must talk to her. It's the future of so many people at stake, after all."

He nodded solemnly. "You are certainly right. I will do that. Whatever happens with Maud, though, I need to find the diamonds if I can. They're part of my family, for good or ill."

"Yes." Flora made herself laugh. "Well, surely we have made a beginning on that? Even if it all seems clear as pond water at the moment. And you have reconnected with your family, and now with your old butler! You can reclaim memories separate from your grandparents. I rather envy that."

He tilted his head. "How so?"

Flora didn't want to talk about the past, to let Benedict know all the terrible things she had done to dig herself up into a new life for herself. She couldn't bear for Benedict, who smiled at her now, looked at her with admiration, know what she had been. What she was. How she recreated memories herself. She glanced out the window and saw they had left London proper, and were headed toward the green spaces of Hampstead. "Are we nearly there? It's been an age since I saw so many trees, so many pretty little gardens! One starts to think the world is made of bricks and stone."

"Yes, nearly. Talbot bought a cottage when he retired. I'm glad to see it looks as if he's living comfortably."

It did indeed look comfortable, Flora thought as

they rolled to a stop outside an iron garden gate. The house was small but pretty, half-timbered with mullion windows, ivy edging up along the walls, blue window boxes filled with splashes of red flowers. Smoke curled invitingly out of the chimney, and neat gravel pathways led through a well-kept garden. Flora wouldn't mind such a place for herself.

As Benedict handed her down, Flora glanced up in time to see a curtain twitch at a window, as if someone watched them arrive. "Aren't retired upper servants usually given a residence on the estate?"

"Yes, as custom. But with the estate's financial woes, I doubt Talbot would have such a well-cared-for residence as this. Or perhaps not one at all, if they must all be rented." He held out his arm to her. "I think he is expecting us."

"Am I your impoverished cousin again?" she whispered as they made their way through the garden gate.

"No, Talbot knows all my family from every side, I'm afraid. You are my—social secretary. Hired by my grandmother to make sure all my books are in order, helping me keep track of my ducal obligations to the staff and estate."

"Oh, I like that! I can be terribly efficient, y'know."

The door swung open before they could knock, and a tall, perilously thin man stood there, his bony face surrounded by sparse strands of cotton-fluff white hair, his bright blue eyes faded as he peered at them. He was immaculately dressed in a butler's black coat, and a delighted smile further creased his deeply lined cheeks.

"Your Grace," he said, trying to make a creaky bow. "What an honor, an honor indeed."

"Not at all, Talbot, you honor me with your invitation. I should have called on you long ago," Benedict said, gently helping the man to rise. "What a great pleasure it is to see you again."

"So kind, Your Grace. Do come in, come in."

The narrow hall was dimly lit, furnished with a carved umbrella stand in the shape of an Indian elephant and a low bench, with a watercolor of green meadows on the maroon-papered wall. Flora wondered if the elephant had been a gift from the duke—or something snatched by Talbot's brother.

"Talbot, may I introduce my new social secretary, Mrs. Forth?" Benedict said. "My grandmother sent her to me to help in organizing the estate, and she is going to be keeping track of staff and tenants, as well as advising me on my social obligations. I need a great deal of help, you see."

"How do you do, Mrs. Forth," Talbot said, leading them toward the sitting room door at the end of the hall. He walked slowly with the aid of a walking stick. "I am very glad to see the estate is getting the attention it deserves at last. It's been much too long since the title was honored as it should be."

"I will do my best to be of assistance," Flora said, stepping through the low door into the waiting room. Like the hall, the sitting room was papered in deep red, the woodwork stained dark, the furniture heavy and carved, upholstered in forest green and gold, looking like cast-offs from the ducal estate. But it was cozy, with a fire in the grate, knitted blankets thrown over the backs of chairs and settees, fringed hassocks for tired feet, a faded but pretty rug underfoot. On the mantel was a display of painted china vases and a few silver-framed photographs. One was of the old duke and duchess, swathed in furs, standing on the steps of what Flora assumed was Thornhill, next to an image of a large staff arrayed on a lawn, a younger Talbot at the forefront.

Another was a faded photograph of a man who looked rather like Talbot, though not quite as tall and heavier, dressed in a very flashy checked suit with pomaded hair. One hand was curled into his lapel, displaying a large, oval, dark-colored stone ring set in filigreed gold. *From Dickon* was scrawled across the bottom. Talbot's felonious brother, she assumed. And strangely, he had six fingers on that beringed hand.

She turned away from the photos as a young maid in a print dress and neat white apron brought in a tea tray.

"I'm so honored you came to call, Your Grace," Talbot said. "How is Thornhill faring? It all seems such a very long time ago, so many fine days there..." His faded eyes seemed to see those far-off times, grand house parties with royalty, the house shining with regality. Flora thought he certainly didn't seem like the sort who would steal jewels from his employers; rather, he appeared a loyal old retainer who saw his work for a ducal household as a glorious thing.

"I fear I've only made one brief visit there of late," Benedict said, smiling at the maid as she handed him a cup of tea and making her blush bright pink. "It's not nearly as well-run as it was under your watchful eye, of course."

Talbot gave a satisfied little smile. "I did fear as much. An estate such as that must have a careful steward at all times. I wish I could return to Thornhill to be of assistance to you, Your Grace, but I am afraid my eyesight is not what it once was. Retirement is all I'm fit for now."

"Oh, but you must be enjoying your time here, Mr. Talbot!" Flora said cheerfully, pouring out more tea. "Your lovely home, seeing your family..."

Talbot gave a deep, mournful sigh. "I fear I have no family left, Mrs. Forth. Aside from a cousin in Maida Vale, she looks in on me from time to time."

"I thought I recalled you had some siblings," Benedict said.

Talbot pursed his lips. "One. Sadly deceased."

"How sad for you," Flora said. She remembered hearing that the thieving brother had vanished; had he since died?

Talbot nodded. "I do fear, Mrs. Forth, that not all families are as they should be. My brother and I were quite different, from our very earliest childhoods, and I'm sure he came to a bad end long ago."

"How did he die?" Benedict asked gently.

Talbot turned away to take a long drink of his tea, as if he was reluctant to say. "I could not say for sure, Your Grace. We ceased contact long before he vanished. Such a waste."

"It sounds much like my own father, sadly," Benedict said.

Talbot shook his head. "Oh, no. Your father was nothing like my own brother, Your Grace! He was a scholar, really, though others thought him a trouble-maker, and I can see he has passed his intellect to you. Tell me, is anyone still at Thornhill from your boyhood?"

As they chattered about the estate, Flora discreetly studied the sitting room for any more clues. Aside from the photographs, the decorations were such as could be found in any respectable house, wax flowers under glass, watercolors of more flowers and sheep in meadows. The bookshelf held leather-bound copies of Dickens and Thackeray, a Georgian silver vase, with one more photo-graph in a carved frame. Flora peeked closer; it looked like Benedict's father, clad in a pale suit, standing on a bridge with a lady in a white dress and large hat, the two of them arm in arm. She looked rather like the tall figure in the Egyptian image, but the swirls of veiling on the hat obscured her face. Drat old fashions!

Mr. Talbot poured out more tea. "You seem inter-ested in my little souvenirs, Mrs. Forth."

"Oh, yes!" Flora exclaimed, and hoped she hadn't been too obviously nosy. "That vase is quite lovely."

"A gift, from your grandfather himself, Your Grace, on the occasion of my retirement," Talbot said. "So kind of him. That man in the photograph there is my poor brother. A fine ring he wears, is it not? A gift, he said, from some admirer." He gave a doubting sniff. "And the other photograph was sent to me by your father, when he was off on his travels. He also sent me this." He reached into a basket beside his chair and took out two small, leather-bound books, the covers faded and water-splotched. "Some writings on those travels. He thought I might be interested in them, I suppose, and knew I would keep them safe. But I fear I can no longer work out the handwriting, even with my spectacles."

He handed the books to Benedict, who took them softly, reverently onto his palm, staring down at them. "These were—my father's?" he said quietly, turning over the worn volumes.

"Oh, yes. And now I give them to you, as I've always meant to." Talbot sat back in his chair, as if weary, and drew a knitted blanket over his legs. "My time at Thornhill was an honor, Your Grace, indeed it was. I am quite grateful to your grandfather for entrusting me with that post, despite—well, despite everything."

"Despite what, Talbot?" Benedict asked, but Mr. Talbot just shook his head and closed his eyes.

"Reputation is everything, is it not?" Talbot said faintly. "If only my own brother had understood that."

It was obvious the old man was very tired, so Benedict and Flora took their leave and made their way back to the carriage. Once they were on their way, Benedict opened one of the journals.

"I can see why Talbot had a difficult time reading this," Benedict said as he carefully turned the yellowed pages. "My father's penmanship was atrocious, and some of it is in pencil which has quite faded."

Flora took a small quizzing glass from her handbag and gave it to him. "Here, try this. It often helps me, as I fear I'm too vain for specs."

Benedict laughed. "But I'm sure they would look absolutely charming on you. I shall use this tonight, and see what I can find in these pages. In the meantime, should we find some dinner? I discovered a nice little Italian cafe, not grand at all but very good."

Flora was sorely tempted to spend as much time as she could with Benedict—and to try some linguine with clam sauce, which she had read about with some interest. But there was work to be done. The landlady always wanted her rent. And she needed to think about what she had seen in Talbot's sitting room, the photographs of his brother and of Benedict's father with the lady in white. "I fear I have another séance this evening."

Benedict studied her for a long, quiet moment, almost as if he was seeking whether to believe her or not. "Of course. Another time. I shall just settle in with a brandy and these books."

And Flora was tempted all over again, by the idea of cozying beside a fire with him, the two of them close together as they solved the puzzle...

Ten

F lora studied the small fortune-teller's tent outside the circus hippodrome. It looked quite different in the gray, drizzly light of day than it had at night. The bright yellows and reds were muted, the streamers hanging limp. The whole area seemed empty and quiet, echoing with the sounds of traffic from the nearby street.

But Flora had woken that morning with strange dreams still swirling around in her head, and she knew somehow that she needed talk to Madame Voronova. She remembered what the woman had said—danger lay ahead. The cord to the past was not yet ready to be cut. Maybe the cards could make some sense of all the strange happenings lately, or maybe Madame Voronova had learned something useful through Mabel. Flora would try anything to get the blasted old duke and his cursed diamonds out of her house! He was disrupting her business and disturbing Chou-Chou. The poor darling hadn't even wanted to get out of bed that morning.

Flora hurried over the tied-down tent entrance and listened carefully for any stirring inside. It was silent, except for a small rusting, a clink like a glass being set down.

"Madame Voronova," she called. "It's Flora Flowerdew. We met a few nights ago, when you did a reading for me? I just have a few more questions."

For a long moment, there was only more silence, and Flora found herself holding her breath. There were other card readers she could go to in London, dozens, maybe even hundreds, but she knew too many of their tricks. Madame Voronova seemed to see—something. Know something.

At last, there was another rustle, a deep breath, and the entrance was thrown back.

Madame Voronova peered out, silvery curls spilling from her turban, her eyes reddened. "I remember you. You were here with that handsome, quiet bloke." No more Russian accent.

"Er—yes," Flora said. Benedict *was* handsome, of course, but quiet? Compared to circus men, probably. "You did a card reading for me."

Madame Voronova frowned. "Yes. I saw danger at your shoulder. Following you."

"I wanted to see if you could do another reading? I have some, well, some small matters that must be cleared up in my life, and I need your help. Your gifts. I could see they were quite rare." A little flattery never hurt when trying to move forward with creative sorts, Flora always found. Also, funds. She held up her beaded handbag.

Madame Voronova studied her for a few seconds longer, before she nodded and stepped back. "I am making tea. Shall you have a cup? I can also read the leaves as well as the cards."

Flora nodded, and wondered if she should also add reading leaves to her own service. Clients might enjoy that. "Thank you."

The tent looked the same, scattered with velvet cushions, smoky with incense, and Madame Voronova's embroidered Chinese robe swept over the dusty carpet. "Sit, sit," she said, waving impatiently toward the table.

She handed Flora a porcelain cup, and they took their places opposite the crystal ball in the center of the fringed cloth. Madame Voronova took her tarot deck from its carved box and gave it to Flora. "Shuffle, please. And drink your tea."

Flora did as asked, and watched tensely as the cards were laid out. But, to her shock, Madame V suddenly went white, and shook her head. "No. I cannot help you any longer. You must go. Now."

"But..." Flora cried, aching to know what the cards held. What she should expect next.

"Go!"

At that shout, Flora realized she had no choice. She fled, with no answers to help her at all.

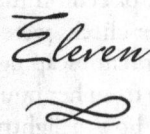

Eleven

The Blue Willow Tea Shop was just the sort of place Regina would choose, Flora thought as she settled herself at a corner table half-hidden by a velvet drape, and drew off her gloves. Cluttered, cozy, filled with sentimental paintings of girls weaving daisy chains and china shepherdesses on curlicued shelves. Maids bustled about in pink dresses and ruffled aprons, serving tea in flowered pots and dainty cakes to whispering ladies.

It was also the sort of place Flora didn't often frequent herself, having few lady friends, and the ones she did have were rather like Evie, who wouldn't be caught dead in such a spot. So she was glad she had arrived a bit early to settle herself into her Miss Fane role. And, she had to admit, it looked like rather a nice place. Maybe she would try tea shops more often.

She glanced into a wavy looking glass framed in exuberant scrolls of gilded ribbons and cupids and straightened her hat, a somber-looking dark brown boater where Mary had removed the feathers and bows. It matched her amber wool walking suit, also denuded of trim. Flora sighed. Being Miss Fane was rather tedious in many ways, not least of which her taste in fashion. But hopefully Regina would let her gossipy side free without her husband looking over her shoulder.

A pot of tea and plate of those scrumptious-looking cakes and scones was placed on the pink tablecloth just as Regina arrived. Her cheeks were as cherry-pink as her dress and parasol, her hair escaping its pins and her eyes wide as if the journey from her house had flustered her.

"Oh, Miss Fane, how delightful to see you again!" she cried, tugging at her parasol handle and trying to unbutton her pink kid gloves. "I am so glad you could meet me."

"I was very grateful to receive your note," Flora answered. "I know so few people in London, and don't really know where to go."

"Oh, I know few people here, too, even though I've lived here for an age! It can be hard to make new acquaintances, and my husband does prefer to lead such a quiet life when he isn't working. Though really, he is gone for work so often, he has so many duties." She studied the array of iced cakes, a smile forming on her lips. "And my father-in-law, though he is quite kind, has his own interests. I run the household, of course, but it doesn't take all my time. I was so sure you and I could be friends from the moment we met!"

Flora felt a terrible pang at deceiving Regina, who did seem so sweet and lonely. She quickly poured two cups of tea and handed Regina the loveliest of the pale green iced cakes. "Have you and your husband always lived with Lord Edward?"

"Oh, yes, since we married years ago! My mother-in-law was alive then, and artists were always coming to the house. I learned so much from her! My own mother was quite an invalid, you see, and I spent much time before I married Lawrence taking care of her. She couldn't teach me how to run a proper house, let alone how to be a ducal connection."

"I am so sorry. It must have been so difficult to watch someone you care about so ill."

"Indeed. She and my father had been in India when they first married. He died there, before I could even remember him, and her health was quite wrecked by the climate." She spooned a helping of sugar into her tea.

India—diamonds. It always did seem to come back to that. "I've heard the heat is quite appalling. Were you yourself much affected?"

Regina shook her head, the plumes on her hat bobbing. "I was sent back to England when I was barely more than a baby, I don't remember it there at all. My mother came back when my father died. He was a doctor, you see, and she the daughter of a colonel, very pretty in her youth. She had stories of their time there, which were quite fascinating but so appalling. Insects and tiger rampages and fevers. And servants you could never trust! But also glorious flowers, she said, such wondrous perfumes."

"Was India what drew you to your husband? There is a family connection there, is there not, with Sir Edward's brother the duke?"

Regina looked shocked. "Oh, no! Lawrence knew so little about my family, I think, and my own parents would not have known the duke and duchess except from afar. We met in Brighton, at a tea dance. I was so astonished to catch the attention of a duke's nephew! I was pretty enough, I suppose, but nothing out of the ordinary. Yet he was so attentive. Back then." She patted at her faded curls, her lips pursed thoughtfully. Wistfully. "Though Edward has always enjoyed hearing about my parents' time in India. I suppose he uses it in his studies, he does spend so much time in his library."

Flora thought of the book hidden in her own room, the one stamped with the ducal crest and the pages underlined. Was Lord Edward, too, searching for something his family had lost? The jewels? "But you are content being there, in that quiet house?"

Regina glanced away. "I am very fortunate. Yet when we first married, Lawrence did say we would have our own establishment when the time was right." She popped another cake into her mouth. "But you must enjoy living in the country on your own, Miss Fane! Or do you, as I did, take care of relatives?"

"No, I have no close relatives now, so I was glad to meet my—my cousin," Flora said. "I have no one to tell me interesting tales of India! How astonishing it must be to see such a place, like the duke's father did. I was intrigued by what you said, that he once had a great romance. How dashing he sounds, just like Lord Emmington in *Dorina's Disgrace!*"

Regina's cheeks flushed rosy, and she fussed with a teaspoon. "Well, I should not have said anything really, as I am not one to gossip. I've always thought it rather interesting that such a person could be related to my own husband! They are so very different."

"Has anyone ever said who that grand love might have been?" Flora said softly, her eyes widened. "Perhaps he met her in his travels. A foreign princess. A maharani!"

Regina leaned forward, her own eyes wide. "I am sure he did meet her on his travels. His poor wife was always at Thornhill, he couldn't have brought anyone near there. I have no idea *who* it could have been, though! I only heard he intended to run away with her, never return. Could it really have been a maharani, do you think? Their portraits do always look so lovely."

"Did your parents know anyone like that in India?"

"Not really. They had their own physicians. Though my mother did say my father once treated a prince for a snakebite, and was given a fine ruby for it! She said he set it in a ring, though I never saw it. And my mother was once presented to the Viceroy! I suppose she might have met people like that in his palace." She glanced at her reflection the mirror, and frowned. "How drab things do seem next to such tales. I often think that was why she grew ill when she left, not the climate! Perhaps she was bored. Though I am quite fortunate in my home and marriage."

"A colorful life isn't so very grand," Flora murmured.

Regina gave her a startled glance. "Do you think not, Miss Fane? We are better off seeing such things only in books?"

"Maybe so." Flora thought of her own youth, the footlights of the stage, the leering men, the spangles and tearful eyes. "Now, should we order some more of those cakes? I do enjoy the raspberry ones so much."

They ate and talked of books and hats, laughing until Flora almost forgot why she was really there. Then the bell on the front door jangled, and she glanced past the half-closed curtain of their little nook to see Maud Petrie and her aunt stepping inside. A maid followed, laden with new hatboxes, though Maud still looked rather wan despite her apparent shopping spree. Her aunt held tightly to her arm, whispering and smiling in a determinedly cheerful way.

Flora started to raise her hand to greet them, but then she remembered she wasn't Madame Flowerdew, but Miss Fane, country cousin. Drat it all! She drew down the brim of her hat and ducked her chin, sinking a bit lower into her chair as the Petries sat down at a table on the other side of the curtain. They were too far away to make out any words, but they did seem to speak most intently to each other. Was Maud confiding in her aunt about her vicarage romance? Or sharing other secrets? Oh, how Flora wished she knew!

❦

Flora stared out at the passing streets through the tram window, not really seeing the shops and parks. She kept going over what she had heard from Regina, and from the Petries. India, marriages, connections she couldn't quite draw out yet.

When she made her way up to her flat, she found the door unlocked and heard laughter and chatter from inside. Worried she might have forgotten an appointment, she rushed to the sitting room.

Mary and Benedict sat by the fire, Chou-Chou on a cushion at their feet, a tea tray and bottle of brandy on the table, the three of them having a hearty chuckle. Flora stood there and watched them for a moment, dumbfounded and happy and scared at how right it all looked, how much like—like coming home to a family.

Fearing she might start crying, she made herself smile and unpinned her hat. "Well, now, I see I am missing quite the party!"

"His Grace was just telling me such a joke," Mary said. "About a chorus girl and a fat old marquess and..."

"Yes," Flora said quickly. "I get the idea, thank you, Mary."

"And we were enjoying a nice brandy! Mary said one of your grateful clients brought it in thanks for finding their lost parakeet," Benedict said, giving her a wide smile that broke her heart even wider open. "Come on, let me pour you some, and you can tell us about your visit with my cousin-in-law. Mary says you met Regina for tea?"

"And you can tell me to what we owe the honor of this call," Flora said, sitting down next to him. She patted Chou-Chou on the head to cover her moist eyes.

Benedict handed her a glass, and held up a book, one of the journals Talbot had given him. "I was just reading this over last night. My father's handwriting was truly terrible, and he seems to use an odd code sometimes, but I've been able to make out a few tidbits. I took some notes, and wanted to see what you think of it all."

Flora scanned the old penciled lines, trying to make out the words. "What does this mean?" she asked. "*The beautiful one has come*. Very pretty. Is it a poem?"

"Perhaps," Benedict said.

"If it is, then he was hardly Tennyson, was he?" Mary said. "Too short."

"I'd wager it's part of that code you mentioned," Flora murmured. "But maybe it *is* just a poem, meant for a specific someone. Regina did say your father had a great romance." She told them what she had learned at tea, about India and maharanis and rubies and Lawrence's financial troubles that kept him from having his own home.

"Maybe Talbot does know more than he was saying," Benedict said. "Surely my father entrusted him with the journals for a reason. We should talk to him again." He pushed himself to his feet.

"What, right now?" Flora cried. "But I just got cozy."

"No time like the present, while it's fresh in our own minds. And the element of surprise!" he held out his hand to her, the tarnished gold signet ring on his smallest finger glinting. "I could take you to dinner after? The Italian cafe?"

"Oh, go on, then, Miss Flora," Mary urged, and Chou-Chou barked agreement.

Flora sighed, and also rose to her feet, taking his hand. "Very well. But I do expect a hearty clam sauce *and* wine, Your Grace."

∿

The cottage looked the same as before, calm and quiet and well-kept, yet Flora felt a strange chill as she studied it. Perhaps it was just all the ghostly goings-on lately that was making her see shadows everywhere, but the windows seemed somehow blank. No smoke was at the chimney, and the garden gate was unlatched and ajar.

Flora glanced up at Benedict, hoping he would give her his wonderfully reassuring smile, but he looked concerned, too. His eyes were narrowed as he studied the house, his arm tense under her hand. It was also getting rather late, the sun setting in a ball of pale gold and pink, and soon it would be dark. They hadn't taken the ducal carriage this time, and the hansom had already gone.

"Perhaps Mr. Talbot isn't at home," she said. She remembered the man's walking stick, his careful frailness and spectacles, and wondered how likely it would be for him to just pop out somewhere.

"Perhaps," Benedict said. He pushed the gate the rest of the way open and started up the path. "Stay behind me, Flora."

She nodded, and swallowed hard past the knot in her throat before she followed him. Ever since she escaped her childhood, always running and ducking from some danger, she had tried her hardest to live her safe and secure. One cranky ghost had upended all that.

But when Benedict reached his hand behind him and she clutched it between her gloved fingers, she didn't feel so frightened after all. Not so very alone.

The front door, like the gate, was slightly ajar. Flora looked down, and saw a footprint on the threshold, which had been so carefully swept and whitewashed before. Ominously dark red, a boot outline. Another print seemed to suggest someone had gone out of the house into the small garden, leaving no marks on the gravel pathway. If someone had taken such a circuitous route out of the cottage, and left the door and gate unlatched...

"Hello? Talbot?" Benedict called, carefully pushing open the door. They crept into the dim hall that led to the sitting room.

Flora shivered. That feeling she had outside became heavier, like a dark cloak settling over her as it had in the séance, muffling the world outside. Things around her grew hazy. Perhaps she was becoming like Chou-Chou, seeing the unseen, which was the last thing she wanted in her life.

She looked up at the beamed ceiling, half-fearing the old duke would be peering down at her, yet there were only shadows.

"Talbot?" Benedict called again. Silence.

The sitting room door was wide open. Benedict stepped to the threshold, and immediately spun around to hold Flora back. "No, Flora, don't go in!"

But she had already seen. Mr. Talbot, slumped sideways in his chair, his glassy eyes unseeing in his gray face. A large stab wound in his chest, surrounded by red, blood dripping onto the floor. The bookshelves, where the journals had resided, was in a mess, volumes all over the place.

Whatever he had known, whatever someone out there wanted hidden—it was all utterly gone now. That poor, poor man.

Twelve

The Channel water was choppy as the ferry rolled toward France, the sky low and pearl-gray, wind whipping past. Most of the passengers had retreated inside, but Flora found that even though she had never been on any water beyond a rowboat on the Serpentine, she felt quite well. Invigorated, even. Free after the previous day's interview with constables, who had seemed quite indifferent to poor Talbot's murder until they discovered they were dealing with a duke. Then they had become entirely obsequious, but still not terribly helpful.

She leaned against the railing, holding onto her hat against the howl of the wind, and laughed at the brisk saltiness of the air.

Chou-Chou huddled beneath a deck chair, shivering despite her new little coat, and glared at Flora. Surely the dog had never been so betrayed.

Benedict laughed, too, but he didn't move from his own deck chair, where a plaid blanket draped his legs and his hat tilted rakishly over one eye. "Are you quite sure you've never traveled before, Flora? You do seem to relish it."

"No, never. When I was younger, I didn't have the coin; now I don't have the time. It's quite glorious!" She waved her gloved hand at the distant banks of clouds. "Is that France?"

"It's too soon to see France, especially in this weather, I'm afraid. But I do have my father's travel journals to keep us entertained." He held up one of the battered leather-bound volumes.

Flora sat down in the chair next to his, and gathered a blanket around herself. Chou-Chou jumped up into her lap as a steward brought warm mulled wine, broth, and plates of biscuits. He asked solicitously if anything else was required. Flora thought it was rather nice traveling with a duke.

"What else does your father say?" she asked, munching a biscuit. "Have you deciphered his shorthand yet?"

"Somewhat, I think. His terrible handwriting is the greater challenge, of course. I suppose that's my one inheritance from him, my headmasters were always complaining about it. He went to Brazil in this chapter, but I couldn't find anything suspicious about his activities there. Just beaches and strange dances, and snakes. Lots of snakes."

"Brazil," Flora sighed. "I would love to see it, snakes or not. Oceans and beaches and cliffs."

"If you want those things, we might have to go to Cornwall, where my father died," Benedict said. "There could be some clues still there, even after so many years. If my grandmother doesn't have any helpful information first."

Flora did love how he said *we*. She'd never been a *we* before. It felt—well, quite nice. She just wished it could last. That this adventure could go on and on. Just with no more murders. She could do well without those.

Yet she knew very well it could not go on. She earned her own crust, a girl from the East End who had been an actress and conducted seances. He was a duke. He was to marry Maud Petrie. That was how the world worked. She just had to store up these memories for future days. And hope the old duke would leave her alone then.

"I doubt Cornwall is quite like Rio de Janeiro," she said. "But I hear it has its own beauties." And its own dangers, like what happened to Benedict's father. Flora shivered and drew the blanket closer.

"This volume talks about his travels to Egypt after South America, apparently after he was in India. I haven't found the Indian sections yet."

"Egypt?" Flora said, remembering the photo of Benedict's father with the two ladies at the pyramids. "Does it mention the grand romance Regina told me about?"

"I'm not sure. Shall we read over a few sections? I'm sure you can help me decipher some of it."

He laid the book out on the small table between them, next to the biscuit plate, and Flora eagerly leaned down to read it. Benedict's cologne, lemony and green and faintly sandalwood, his laugh near her ear, was dashedly distracting, making her head swim like too much champagne. But Flora shook away her dreamy thoughts and focused on the written words. The handwriting was indeed terrible, faded and scrawling like a spider, yet she found as she concentrated she could make out the sentences. There were also sketches, pyramids and statues and sandy dunes.

And one lady, her face half-turned away, her long hair veiling her profile except for the glimpse of a half-smile. One hand was raised, rings glinting on her long fingers, a large, square dark stone on the center finger just like in the photograph.

"I've been able to decipher some of the words my father transposes for other words, see," Benedict said. "It's a simple enough code, he wasn't exactly Francis Walsingham, but it's not consistent at all. See, in these sections he doesn't even seem to have a code at all."

"And yet these parts are readable," Flora said, pointing out some short paragraphs that mixed sketches of hieroglyphics with regular words. "Who is Nefertiti? Is she a code name? She certainly seems to appear too often to be a tourist site."

"His great love? The woman in this sketch? Perhaps, yes. Listen to this. *Our kiss on the banks of the Nile was like magic, fated. We have been like this for centuries, I am sure. Nothing can hold us apart now... Like a novel.*"

Flora sat back and stared out at the gray waves, turning over thoughts of Egypt and romance and jewels in her mind. "It's fascinating. What an unusual man your father must have been! Hardly like his own father at all. But was it worth killing poor Mr. Talbot to keep him from showing this to us? For ransacking his shelves looking for it?"

Benedict frowned thoughtfully. "Maybe it wasn't really the journals. Unless he promised them to someone else, or was keeping them for them?"

"For his criminal brother? We're not even really sure how Talbot came to have them, though he said it was from your father," Flora said. "Or maybe he told us something he should not have, or was about to tell us, and someone found out."

"It seems I've never really known my family at all," Benedict said, quietly, sadly.

Flora's heart ached for him, and she squeezed his hand. "I'm sure your grandmother can tell us more."

Benedict laughed, and drew away to pour more wine. "My grandmother is a steel trap when she doesn't want to speak of something—and there is a great deal she doesn't speak about, ever. Though I haven't seen her in a long time. Perhaps she has grown mellow with age."

"Or perhaps she won't notice so much if we dig about the place," Flora said. "Who am I meant to be this time?"

"Perhaps we could be inspired by your friend Evie?

You are a lady reporter, researching a history of the glorious Everton title!"

"Oh, yes, that could be fun," Flora said with satisfaction. "All about their stately homes, their royal service. No scandals, of course. And it would certainly excuse my asking questions!"

"And a lady reporter wouldn't be expected to have a chaperon or maid."

"I do have Chou-Chou." Flora kissed her doggy nose, and Chou-Chou snuggled deeper into the blanket. "But your grandmother might suspect a bit of skullduggery anyway."

"If she does, she'll only care if it's indiscreet. That's the real motto of the Evertons—do what you want, but never get caught. That was my father's problem, of course. He didn't care if he got caught." He looked down at the book with a rather wistful expression. "Maybe if he had been more discreet, he wouldn't have come to such an ending."

Flora gently touched his hand. "We're going to find the answers, I know it."

He smiled at her, and it was as if the sun broke through those gray clouds. "Of course we are. You can do anything, Flora Flowerdew. Now, what do you think about this page here? It seems my father went to see a tomb opening at Amarna, and he mentions Nefertiti again..."

Thirteen

A s the small, open carriage climbed slowly,
creakily up a steep, rocky roadway along the
side of a scrubby, green-gray hill, Flora
couldn't help but stare open-mouthed at the scene
around her. Sapphire-blue sea to one side, far below,
crashing against the rocks like frothing tulle. Cliffs and
ledges raising sharply to the other side, holding up white
and candy-colored villas that looked just like enormous
tea-cakes.

Unlike gray, fog-bound, depressing London, the sky
was azure, dotted with cottony little clouds, and the
breeze smelled of flowers and salt spray. The carriages
that dodged past them, oblivious to the narrow space,
were filled with ladies in silk and lace, feathered little
hats, dainty parasols, chiming laughter as they leaned
close to their handsome companions in Savile Row
suits. It was all so perfect. Flora just hoped no angry
ghosts could follow them there.

She straightened her plain dark blue hat, newly
trimmed with Parisian cherry-red satin streamers, and
tilted her own parasol against the dazzling sunlight,
telling herself she was just as tastefully dressed as anyone
else there. Though she couldn't quite believe it, as a
young lady with guinea-gold curls swept past in a rosy-

pink Worth carriage dress and gauzy picture hat. Even the poodle settled on her lap sported a matching pink jacket. Chou-Chou gave a wistful sigh to see it, and laid her head sadly on her paws. She only had her little wool travel coat.

Benedict didn't seem to notice Flora's sartorial plainness, though. His bright head was bent over the notes he held in his hand, a little frown creased between his eyes. He didn't look at the beauty all around them, whether it be ladies or sea and sky.

"How long has it been since you saw your grand-mother?" she asked.

"Oh," Benedict said, making a pencil mark on one of the papers, still distracted. "I saw her at my grandfather's funeral, soon after I returned to England. I thought it would take her a long time to decide to leave Thornhill, it had been her home for so long, but she was already half-packed and ready to leave for France. She had been to a house party at this house once, and found that her friend who owned it now wanted to sell. She said she didn't want to miss out on the chance, and had never cared for the dower house."

Flora glanced around at the tall, graceful cypress trees, the rush and ebb of the sea, the fresh, green smell of the air. She imagined an old ducal dower house, crumbling old stone and dark corridors. "I can't say I blame her."

Benedict laughed. "I think she just didn't want to see the changes I might make. The way she thought I would ruin Thornhill. End the true Everton ways."

"What changes have you made, then?"

"Not much as of yet. I do have lots of ideas, but such things do take money."

"Hmm, yes." Flora reminded herself sternly that was why they were there; Benedict needed money, and Maud Petrie had it—if Benedict's grandfather would end his interfering. After that was all done and dusted, Flora wouldn't see Benedict any longer. Once the diamonds were found and returned, and the old duke was convinced the "curse" was lifted...

But before anything else, the diamonds *did* have to be found. And the list of people who might have some idea of where they were was dwindling fast. Poor Mr. Talbot.

Flora was suddenly struck with a chilling thought. "Benedict. Do you think your grandmother is quite safe? After we talked with Mr. Talbot, he ended up— you know..."

He frowned. "The constable said it was a robbery."

"It looked like it, with those shelves turned over, but do you believe it? Mr. Talbot had lived there peacefully for years with no troubles, unless he was lying about his brother never visiting. And it seemed he had little valuable to steal. That silver vase was still there. Perhaps someone found out he had your father's journals, but didn't know we had taken them away."

"You think someone saw us go there?"

Flora thought of the quiet streets outside the cottage. "I'm not sure yet. Possibly. Or maybe they were friends with Mr. Talbot, and he just mentioned we had visited. So, your grandmother..."

"My grandmother is always surrounded by people, unlike Talbot. I doubt anyone could get through her phalanx of staff. And she doesn't trust anyone. But I will try to give her a warning, keep a subtle eye out while we're there."

Flora studied the tall, steel-tipped garden gates of a villa they were passing. Houses here did seem impregnable, but thieves were too clever. The high-class ones, anyway. She had met plenty of foolish pickpockets in her time. "If she doesn't trust anyone, how can we persuade her to really talk to us? Especially me, a supposed reporter."

He smiled merrily, an enticing little dimple low in

his cheek. It was quite unfair to a girl's sensibilities, how adorable he could be. "Because you are not a reporter like your friend Evie. You write about Society. You *love* fashion and titles and royalty, and are in awe of the great history and dignity of the Everton title. So much so that you feel called to use your research to make sure their heroic deeds are known to posterity. You are very, very honored by Her Grace's kind invitation."

Flora giggled to remember all the rehearsals they had on the boat and the train, preparing her for just this role. She knew far more about Benedict's family back to Tudor times than she really cared to, and it was all jotted down in a thick notebook tucked into her valise. In her opinion, the family was lucky to have lasted so long, given that they were full of characters like Elizabethan privateers and Georgian gamblers.

"If only I'd had such a part at the Follies!" she said. "I would have been the ingenue of the season."

"So what kind of parts *did* you play? Portia? Juliet?"

Flora stared even harder at the landscape, trying to force away any memories of dancing in a chorus dressed in spangled tights, or waving a feather duster about as a saucy chambermaid. And her big break, as Miss Shambleshanks, the gold digging fiancée of a fake prince in *Tennis For Two*. "Oh, not much Shakespeare or Moliere. I never studied hard enough or stayed at one theater long enough to get that far. I found my best part with Chou-Chou's help!" The director's wife of *Tennis for Two* had loved dogs, and begged Flora to give Chou-Chou to her. By the time the woman realized Flora would never give up her pup, the part was past.

"Finding granny's garnet brooches and lost cats?"

"People do love their cats. Chou-Chou and I are glad to help. But I might have..." Her words trailed away, and she shook her head. It was too embarrassing to admit she once cherished such dreams.

Benedict tilted his head to watch her curiously. "Might what?"

"I might have really enjoyed playing Portia. Or at least giving it a try."

The carriage slowed, and turned in at an open pair of elaborate wrought iron gates, formed of twining vines and flowers, tipped with gilded pyramids that glittered in the sunlight. The lane widened into a manicured driveway, lined with towering cypress trees, with gardens glimpsed beyond. Fruit trees and paths of roses interspersed with white marble statues of gods and goddesses, cupids, bubbling fountains. In the distance, Flora saw a large greenhouse, and a summerhouse folly with a mosaic rotunda roof.

Around a sharp curve, the Villa d'Or was reached at last. Flora gasped a bit at the sight, she just couldn't help it. It was like a palace in a fairy-tale book, a backdrop of a romantic play. All towers and mansard roofs, white stones and chimneys, with hundreds of diamond-glittering windows. The drive curved in a large circle around a burbling fountain crowned with Artemis, poised with bow aloft, and led to a double flight of stone steps. Topiaries in the shapes of heraldic creatures shaded the way.

The front doors at the top of the steps opened, and a black-clad pair of butler and housekeeper appeared, followed by long double rows of footmen and housemaids. Benedict was right, Flora realized—the duchess was well-guarded here. So many people to look after one old lady.

"How does your grandmother afford all this if the Everton estate is in trouble?" Flora whispered. "You said her jointure isn't large."

Benedict studied the villa, his face unreadable. "It's not, as such things go. Perhaps she had some inheritance apart from the Evertons, from her own family. Her father was an earl, and she was his only daughter."

Or perhaps the duchess was selling family treasures, Flora thought. It wasn't rare, ladies of old families exchanging family jewels for paste. Surely the lady was owed *something* after years putting up with the old duke. But surely the old duke himself wouldn't be happy at all if his wife was selling the diamonds.

As the carriage rolled to a stop at the foot of the steps, two footmen in sky-blue livery and powdered hair, just like they were at old Versailles, rushed to open the carriage door. The butler and housekeeper followed at a more sedate pace, frowning when they glimpsed Chou-Chou in Flora's arms. Perhaps the duchess's famous Pekingese didn't like new friends.

"Monsieur le duc," the butler said with a low bow. "And Mademoiselle Fine, *oui*? Madame la duchesse is expecting you. I am Lumiere, butler here, and this is Madame Valliere. You are quite welcome."

"*Merci*," Benedict said. They followed the dour pair up the stone steps, past the curtsying and bowing ranks of servants, who watched them with curious eyes until a sharp word from Madame Valliere made them glance away.

Inside the doors, the warm, bright day fell away, and the temperature dropped sharply. Chou-Chou shivered against Flora's jacket sleeve. The foyer soared high above a twisting staircase to a stained-glass dome, but the walls, the floor and the carved marble pillars were all in cold, pale stone. It was bare of furniture except for a pair of suits of armor flanking an empty fireplace, and two medieval painted chests. Dark blue velvet draperies covered the windows.

"Is Henry VIII about to come out and order us to the Tower?" Flora whispered. Benedict covered a laugh behind a cough.

Monsieur Lumiere tossed them a disdainful glance, as if laughing was not allowed here. "If you will follow me, Madame la duchesse awaits."

They went up the stairs, up and up, and Flora felt as if they would end in that dome. Luckily there was a thick, faded, flowered carpet on the old stair treads to give some warmth, and paintings on the pale blue walls as well as niches holding medieval sculptures of saints fighting dragons to distract. Flora gaped at all the lolling goddesses and disapproving men in velvet doublets who stared down at her from their gilded frames. Even she could recognize Raphael, Rubens, Holbein. The duchess had some money coming from *somewhere*.

They finally reached a doorway, which the butler silently opened to reveal an enormous drawing room. Unlike the stony foyer, it was the image of plush luxury, settees and chairs upholstered in blue and gold brocade, velvet draperies at the tall windows, fresh flowers in alabaster and crystal vases on every table, more paintings, more goddesses.

And a full-length portrait of the duchess herself over the massive marble fireplace, proud and grand in black satin and the full panoply of the diamonds.

The real thing rose from an armchair by the crackling grate, just as tall, just as dignified, but dressed in a chiffon and silk tea gown and pearls rather than diamonds. Her hair was almost as dark as in the painting, just touched with a bit of silver at the temples, her blue eyes chilly. She held out a hand decorated with emeralds and amethysts.

"Benedict. My dear," she said diffidently. She glided across the pink and sky-blue carpet, the lacy train of her gown twisting behind her, a Pekingese trotting along like a moving footstool. "How lovely to see you at last. How very busy you have been of late!"

Benedict dutifully kissed her powdered and rouged cheek, or rather the air just above it as she held back a bit, as if to keep that careful layer of paint from mussing. "Indeed. Thornhill and Everton House need a great deal of supervision, Grandmama."

She sighed, and waved the embroidered handkerchief in her hand on a cloud of violet scent. "They are in a sad state, I fear, since your grandfather last had his firm hands on the reins! But you are there at last, that is what matters. A duke's steady eye is needed there at all times. And a *duchess* is even more important. I was *worshiped* at Thornhill, and that kept everything just as it should be. I have heard that you have been seen about London with a young lady." She cast that chilling blue gaze over Flora. "This, I think, is not her."

"Grandmama, this is the Society column reporter I told you about in my letter," Benedict said. "Miss Fine. She is deeply interested in the history of the Evertons."

"Oh, yes?" the duchess answered doubtfully.

"Yes! Oh, Your Grace, I cannot tell you how very excited I am to be here, to meet you at last," Flora gushed. She reminded herself 'eyes wide, smile bright.' "I am particularly interested in the third and the seventh dukes, and your own husband, of course. All their brave deeds in battle, and such sterling service to the Crown!"

The duchess's powdered mask of an expression softened, and she even smiled. "Of course, their stories are quite legendary. What fascinating work you must have, Miss—Fine, is it? I believe Benedict mentioned you have also written a great deal about the Steel-Smythe and the Camberton families."

"Yes, indeed." Flora hoisted Chou-Chou up in her arms as the Pomeranian started to growl low in her throat at the inquisitive Peke. "In fact, the Marchioness of Camberton was the one who gifted me with my precious puppy in thanks for the work I did on their history! But *your* family is so much more distinguished than them. It will be my very best work by far."

"Aren't you sweet. And a *working* lady, my heavens, so modern. I should have been a very fine writer myself, if I had attempted a novel. My friends say my letters quite transport them." She took Benedict's arm and turned back toward the fireplace, and her own painted image. "Do sit down, have some tea, and tell me how I may be of assistance."

They seated themselves around the fire, near a round, marble-topped table laden with luscious-looking French eclairs and pastel macarons, as well as the Meissen tea service and silver pot. Embroidered cushions softened the seats, and cashmere throws were tossed carelessly over their backs. Flora even noticed eighteenth century chests and side tables that looked as if they must come from Versailles. Chou-Chou joined her new friend the Peke on a canopied dog bed in the corner, swagged with satin and gold tassels. Yes, money was somewhere here.

Benedict and the duchess chatted of the Everton houses, of the duchess's friends in London, while Flora munched on a pearl-pink macaron and studied that portrait of the duchess, the shining diamonds of the tiara, necklace, and earrings, Indian peacock feather fans arched over her head, shadowy figures in saris behind her. No one noticed the dogs stealing two petit-fours.

"What a very exquisite portrait, Your Grace," Flora said when the conversation lulled. "In India, I am sure. Everyone speaks of how your husband did such glorious work there."

The duchess smiled. "Oh, yes. The gardens at one of the palaces of Hyderabad. Mr. Neill was the artist, as you can tell, he came all the way to India to paint me. The diamonds sparkle to the life." She sighed happily, her blue eyes gazing far into the past. "My husband was truly a great man, you know, Her Majesty's most valuable advisor, especially in India. The place was never so perfectly run as when he was there." She turned away, her lips pressed together. "He was robbed, absolutely robbed, of his rightful position as Viceroy. It was a blow to all our hard work! But then, England needed us as well. You will, I am sure, my dear Miss Fine, want to hear all about our work at Thornhill. It was in a shocking condition after his father died. It is a great sadness you will not meet my dear husband. A great man indeed. A vast loss to Her Majesty."

Flora thought of the duke roaring around her séance room, trying to scare Chou-Chou then running off to his celestial card games. She tried not to roll her eyes, and took another macaron.

Benedict popped a sugared almond into his mouth. "You haven't heard from dear old Grandfather, by any chance, Grandmama?" he said casually.

The duchess looked at him as if he'd just bit off her Pekingese's squashed nose. "Heard from your grandfather? The man has been dead for an age. You aren't beginning to suffer in your brain as your father did, are you, Benedict?" She moaned softly, and buried her face in her handkerchief. "Oh, not the Everton curse again! I could not bear it. Our lives ruined once more ..."

"Of course not, Grandmama. It just seems that table-tipping and sorts of things like that are all the rage in London right now. I just wanted to know if he'd been heard around lately."

"Of course he has not. Your grandfather was a gentleman. He would not do something so ill-bred as to tip a table." She peered at Benedict doubtfully, as if she could see into a disordered brain.

"But you must have glorious memories of your life together, Your Grace!" Flora said, reminding herself to be perky and enthusiastic and ingratiating. She was a Society reporter who *loved* royalty, which really didn't sound like such a bad job. "And the gifts he gave you! How magnificent you look in those diamonds."

The duchess's icy eyes thawed as she studied the painted tiara. "Indeed. He had the finest taste, and a true instinct for what an event called for. The Everton diamond parure surpassed even the Vicereine's. They became our great trademark."

"I should so love to see you wear them," Flora said.

The duchess turned sharply away, her hand trembling as she reached for the teapot. "I fear that will never again be possible. They were cruelly stolen, by my own son! Such calumny. I am very sorry to have to speak of it, Miss Fine."

Flora gasped, and pressed her hands dramatically to her cheeks. Benedict looked as if he might laugh, and she wondered if she had gone a bit too far. "How very dreadful. Did he sell them?"

The duchess dabbed at her eyes with her handkerchief. "Worse, my dear. He had one of his insane notions that the diamonds belonged in India and should be restored there. He had spent many years traveling, you know, and had such—odd notions."

"Did the late duke obtain the jewels from some Indian maharajah, then? Someone who wanted them back?"

"No, indeed. They had been bought by an English family before us, *long* before us, from the Maharajah of Sharma. His dear first wife had just died, I think, and he couldn't bear to see another wear them, let alone dismantle them. So he sold them to a wealthy merchant named—Porter, I think? Potter? No, Stillroom. Stilton? A man who had ideas above his station, no doubt. The maharajah's mother was angry, they say, and put a curse on the stones. Such nonsense one did hear in India! Benedict, you wouldn't believe the ridiculous superstitions. This, I am sure, cannot be important to your story, Miss Fine. A mere aberration in the family history."

Flora nodded. "So you bought them from this—Mr. Potter, Your Grace? Such an honor that must have been for him."

"My husband did buy them, yes, for a very fair price. The pieces were in such need of cleaning and resetting to restore them to their true glory, not to mention a wearer worthy of them." She sighed again as she looked at her portrait. "Perhaps it is best they were gone. Poor Isabel, so thin and pale, she never could hope to even stand up beneath them."

"So they were cursed before the theft?" Flora asked.

"Mr. Potter's wife, Henrietta I think was her name, or Harriet. No, that wasn't it at all, it was a strange, old-fashioned name. She died before she could wear them, after she sold them to us. Their little daughter was shipped off back to England. No, Stillworth was the name! I do recall now. Such a shame. I think he was a secretary, or maybe a lawyer. Something medical?"

"But the curse never troubled you, did it, Grandmama?" Benedict said.

The duchess waved this off with a flutter of her jeweled hand. "I would never let it, would I? Willpower, that is what the Everton ladies require. And common sense not to believe such claptrap." She leaned toward Benedict and said darkly, "I do hope that whatever young lady you have your eye on, Benedict, possesses just such willpower."

"I am quite sure she does," Benedict said softly.

Flora thought of Maud Petrie and her tears over her vicar, and shook her head. But the Stillworth family, that was intriguing indeed. Could the unfortunate family who sold them possibly have been Regina's?

The duchess poured more tea. "It is too sad we shall not see her in the diamonds at the next coronation. Though, truly, what a disgraceful spectacle that is bound to be! Bertie is so very shocking..."

As they finished their tea and talked of the news of the royal family, the gilded clock on the fireplace mantle chimed, tiny enameled cupids fluttering around the ivory face. "You must be tired, Miss Fine," the duchess said. "I have put you in the Rose Room, I shall have the first box of documents for your research sent up to you. Feel free to use the library, as well, though I think most of our papers are at Thornhill. I do live a much quieter life here. Dinner, you will find, is shockingly early at seven. But we are in for a treat! The new Maharajah of Sharma's nephew is in France, and is hosting a party at the casino tomorrow. Nothing grand, he assures me, our casino is *tres petite*, yet you might hear one or two tales of our Indian days to add to your story. The Everton title is still so revered there. And here I am, sadly left in penury."

The duchess rang a bell, and a stone-faced maid in gray poplin appeared. "Your Grace?" she said, in a distinctly London accent.

"Ah, Henderson." So no French maidservants for the duchess. "Do show Miss Fine to the Rose Room. Benedict, shall we stroll in the garden for a time?"

Flora collected Chou-Chou from her tete-a-tete with her new friend, made her curtsy, and followed Henderson out of the drawing room. They went back down the grand staircase to another corridor, lined with closed doors. It was hushed and dim in the late afternoon light, and Flora wished she could hear what the duchess was saying to Benedict in the garden.

Maidservants were just finishing unpacking Flora's valises, and she was glad she had brought her best tucker with her for chateau dinners and casino parties. She tucked Chou-Chou against the pink cushions of the bed, and glanced at the crates of papers that had been delivered.

"Shall you require anything else, Miss Fine?" the stony Henderson asked, and Flora worried that the woman's stolid eyes could see through everything. Every bit of this masquerade.

"Oh, no, this looks beautiful," Flora said hastily, nudging at Chou-Chou when she showed too much interest in a pink and gold tassel hanging from the bed-curtains.

Henderson's lips pursed. "Very well. Remember,

137

miss, dinner at seven exactly. First gong at six. A bath will be sent up, and Yvette can help you with your dress."

Yvette. So the staff hadn't come wholesale from London. "Thank you very much."

Henderson sniffed and departed, and Flora was left alone to snoop about a bit. Not in the whole villa yet; staff were surely scurrying about the place in daylight, and it seemed as big as the Bank of England. But her own chamber seemed a good place to start.

She tucked the pink satin blankets around Chou-Chou, unpinned her hat, and looked about. She'd never had a place so large to herself! The tiny flat where she was born would have fit in the little alcove where the dressing table sat, her brushes and perfume bottle set out for her. The whole room was like a giant pink cloud, pink rug, pink curtains, pink marble fireplace. Only the plain brown boxes of papers were anything other than a shade of rose.

She went to peek out the window, past the pink and white striped silk draperies, and studied the garden below. A little white stone folly sat atop a rise, watching over the rose beds and gravel pathways, the towering cypresses shading little groves and nooks. The duchess and Benedict strolled past, her hand tight on his arm, her face solemn as she talked and talked and he nodded and nodded.

Flora frowned as she examined the elaborate gardens. She couldn't figure out how someone left in "penury" as the duchess claimed (though of course, there was *real* poverty and there was aristocratic poverty, where a French villa equaled a pensioner's squat), could possibly live there. Benedict said her jointure was not large, and her own family had not been wealthy, being of old name but tiny stock portfolios, and she had refused the Thornhill dower house.

Flora ran her fingers over a small marble sculpture of

Cupid and Aphrodite on a stand next to her. Bellini, if she wasn't mistaken, and the villa was stuffed with such things. Yet Benedict needed the Petrie money to keep his roof on the house.

Very strange. Where did Her Grace get all the cabbage? Selling jewels, maybe?

Flora turned away toward the papers in the crates. Cor, more papers. Would she ever get away from them? Or more to the point, would they ever tell her anything important?

She glance at Chou-Chou, who had fallen asleep on her back in the silken embrace of the pink blankets. Her paws stuck straight up, and she was snoring.

"Easy life for some," she grumbled, and opened the first batch of papers. Letters from the time of the second duke, they were labeled. She sneezed as a great cloud of dust went up.

～

"...such an exciting life you have led, Your Grace," Flora exclaimed, for what felt like the one hundredth time since they sat down to dinner. The villa's dining room was lovely, all gold and cream sparkling under several Venetian glass chandeliers, with tall, open doors looking out to the moonlit gardens. The food was extraordinary, too, delicate fishes and vegetables in creamy French sauces.

But Flora had forgotten how exhausting fawning over one other person could be, keeping up a persona for a whole evening. She'd hoped she'd left that behind with her Follies days. Séances with customers only lasted an hour.

Yet there was no other way to get the duchess to talk. She was too wary, too wily, too skilled in years of diplomacy. Flora rather admired her steely spine. Luckily, the duchess was also spoiled and rather self-centered, and had no surprise that someone wanted to hear all about who she had met in royal palaces and at long-ago tea parties. Flora didn't learn about the duchess's financial accounts, of course, but she did hear all about presentations at Court, polo games, and weekends at Balmoral.

She glanced across the table at Benedict, who flashed her a quick, conspiratorial smile. How difficult it must have been, Flora thought, growing up with such people! He had all the things she did not as a child—food, warmth, education. But his parents were gone, his grandparents cold and controlling. How had he ended up as he had, with kindness and easy humor in his heart? She wished she knew.

She nodded and smiled at the duchess, listening to the end of a story about Derby Days in the royal box as the dessert of a lovely charlotte russe was finished. "Tell me, my dear Miss Fine, have you found much of interest in the documents I sent up?" the duchess asked. "I fear I've had little time to peruse them myself, though I hope one day to use them to write my memoirs."

Flora sighed inwardly to think of the large crates of very dusty volumes waiting up in the Rose Room. Being a detective sounded so amusing, but really it was paperwork! She feared she had a long night of reading ahead of her. "Oh, yes. Quite fascinating. I am deep into a sketchbook of Court gowns right now, quite stunning." That, at least, was true. The dresses were gorgeous.

"I'm so glad you will be able to make use of it in your writing. My husband was indeed such a vital man in the life of the nation." She turned to her grandson. "You have been rather quiet tonight, Benedict."

He smiled at her. "Just listening to your glorious tales, Grandmama. Miss Fine is right, it is all fascinating. And I am enjoying this grand dinner. Your arrangements are as elegant as ever."

She gestured around, at the Hepplewhite sideboard

laden with silver and fresh flowers, the paintings, the chandeliers. "I live quietly, Benedict. So very different from my younger days! But suitable, I fancy, for an old dowager such as myself. There must be room for a new duchess to make her mark. Shall we take our coffee on the terrace? It's a beautiful evening."

She led them through the open doors onto the marble terrace, where a table had already been laid out with the silver coffee service and plates of petit-fours and chocolates. After an hour of chatting more about the Everton genealogy, gossip about local Society, the duchess bid them a good evening and Flora was left alone in the magical garden with Benedict.

"I am sure you see what I see here, Flora," Benedict said, nodding at the gloriously torchlit villa, the gardens glowing under the French stars.

"How does she pay for this life?" Flora examined the trees, swaying in the salty-sea wind. "It is beautiful, though. I wouldn't mind a little place like this. Or such gardens. Smell those roses!"

Chou-Chou barked as she chased a butterfly down one of the white graveled paths, and Flora and Benedict laughed together. It *was* a rather magical place, she couldn't blame the duchess for wanting it no matter what.

"CC would enjoy it, too, I think," Benedict said.

"So she would. I do wish I had a garden for her."

They watched in silence for a moment, the dog gamboling in the beautiful flowerbeds, the moonlight. "Where did you meet Chou-Chou?"

"I found her behind a trash tip one night," Flora said softly. She didn't tell him about how hungry she was that night, how cold and lonely. How lost. And the sudden flash of hope when she heard that little yap... "She'd obviously been on her own for a few days, I don't know where she came from. But she was thirsty and skinny, poor love, and so dirty. You could barely tell what color she was! I thought she might bite me when I came close to her, but she just toddled out to me and fell against me, like she knew I would help her. I could barely help myself then, but knowing she believed in me —I could suddenly believe in myself. Believe I could take care of us both. That's when I had the idea of Madame Flowerdew. It was a bit of a slow start, once I left the theater, but I met Mary, and she and Chou-Chou helped me along. And here we are! Now she's spoiled beyond belief."

The duchess's Pekingese, who had come out to find Chou-Chou, yapped and fell over in a stand of lavender, while Chou-Chou dashed away, barking. Benedict gazed down at Flora, his face expressionless but his eyes tender. "Well, spoiled or not she seems to get more exercise than my grandmother's dog. I am sure you'll have a fine garden for her very soon. You both deserve that."

"None as grand as this, though." She watched as Benedict leaned on the marble balustrade. "Are you really thinking she might have been the one to steal the diamonds? To add to her small jointure?"

"She had to find the funds somehow. It's difficult to see how, though. Or how her pride would have let her. Have you come across any accounts in those papers? I had a quick look through the library, but there was nothing."

"Not yet. Just sketches of gowns and invitations to royal banquets. Your grandmother doesn't strike me as being someone so careless as to just leave her financial accounts lying about in storage boxes, especially if there's something hinky about them."

"No, indeed. We might have to dig a bit more through the library. I do remember my grandfather had a desk with locking drawers, if she brought it with her." He glanced up at the windows of the bedchamber floor. The largest suite of rooms, with tall windows looking over the garden from two sides, were surely the duchess's, glowing gold with light and warmth.

It seemed to watch Flora, to know everything she kept secret. The armor around her heart. The loneliness that had plagued her before she met CC; the loneliness she saw flashing in Benedict's eyes sometimes. Oh, yes. She truly needed to strengthen that armor, and fast.

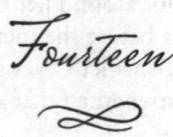

Fourteen

The duchess had called the casino *tres petit*, but Flora thought it could never be called "small" at all. Small compared to Versailles, maybe, but perhaps about the same as Kensington Palace. The parade of rooms—gaming rooms, ballrooms, a music room—were draped in scarlet brocade and silver-framed mirrors that reflected the lavishly-dressed and bejeweled crowds on and on into the chandelier sparkle.

It wasn't as crowded as Flora imagined it would be at the height of the season, but there were still plenty of clusters of people in their pastel silks and perfectly-cut evening suits. They laughed together on velvet banquettes, leaned over the roulette wheel and frowned at hands of cards, swirled in waltzes to the music of the orchestra. Through the half-open glass doors, Flora glimpsed couples strolling along the terrace between banks of potted palms.

She glanced up at the man beside her, Benedict, the most handsome of all, his hair shimmering in the candlelight. This was his world, his true place. And one day, when this was over, he would vanish into it and she would be gone.

But not tonight. Not yet. There were a few adventures yet to have.

"Hmm, a quiet evening," the duchess said as she handed her ermine-edged cape to a footman. "I don't see anyone I know."

Flora removed her own, more modest wrap, and followed the duchess and Benedict through the foyer and a refreshment room where champagne and peach ices were being served. She hardly recognized herself when she caught a glimpse in one of the floor-to-ceiling mirrors. A subdued gown of lavender organza, her hair drawn back and threaded with flowers from the duchess's fine garden. And Benedict beside her.

"Madame la duchesse," a man called out, and a portly figure in a scarlet waistcoat and with a sparkling monocle propped on his round face, rushed forward to bow over the duchess's gloved hand. "How very happy I am to see you in our modest rooms tonight. The whist tables have been empty without you."

"Nonsense, Monsieur Valmont. You get along very well without my modest stakes," the duchess said briskly. Flora noticed she glanced away and fiddled with a diamond bracelet draped over her glove, and she wondered if the duchess often lost those "small" stakes. "Benedict, this is Monsieur Valmont, the concierge of the casino, our master of ceremonies. Monsieur, my grandson, the Duke of Everton. And Miss Fine, a writer for an English newspaper, who has come to observe my quiet little corner for a time."

"Ah, monsieur le duc, you are most welcome indeed. Madame la duchesse speaks of you so often." He gave a low, courtly bow. "And Mademoiselle Fine, such an honor you would wish to see our small society. I should be most happy to answer any questions."

"Thank you, monsieur," Flora said, as if shy and breathless. She hoped it sounded that way, anyway. "Your rooms are so beautiful."

"You are here for the maharajah's party, no?" Monsieur Valmont said, and offered his arm to the duchess. "It is in the Garden Room, let me escort you there."

The Garden Room lived up to its name, lavishly decorated with floral brocade on every chair and settee, enormous arrangements of roses and lilies on every table, carved wreaths twining around mirrors and doorways. A large buffet sat along the far wall, piled with delicacies, and another buffet held champagne and claret. A laughing crowd gathered around a tall, darkly handsome young man, merry and loud.

Flora was a tiny bit disappointed that the maharajah didn't wear a bejeweled turban, but a perfectly ordinary black and white evening suit, with just one very large, very fine pearl pinning his starched neckcloth. But he *was* quite handsome, tall and slim, with liquid brown eyes. And he was surrounded by an equally handsome crowd, all satins and diamonds and laughter.

"Ah, the Duchess of Everton," the maharajah said, and his voice sounded as if he had just stepped off a cricket pitch at Oxford, rich and sparkling as cut-glass. "I have heard much of your days in India from my father. How charming to meet you at last. Do you know my friends, the Essex-Bridewells? The Marquis Duvall? And my secretary and old friend, Mr. Patel."

"Of course, all except Mr—Patel, is it?" the duchess said, nodding as the man next to the maharajah gave her a bow. "So nice to see you all again. I quite feel nostalgic after seeing you, my dear maharajah. Our days in India, alas..."

As the duchess again spoke of how indispensable her darling late husband was to the Empire, Flora quietly slipped away to take a few delicacies from the buffet and observe the people around her. Eavesdropping was always so very useful.

With her lavishly-laden plate, she found a quiet seat in a corner and took her notebook out of her evening purse. She was a newspaper writer, after all; it would make sense for her to take notes, and she didn't want to miss any possible clues. She jotted down who was at the party and what she hoped to learn from the maharajah about the diamonds, as she nibbled on the apricot tarts.

"I beg your pardon, mademoiselle, but are you the writer they say is researching the Evertons?" a man said softly.

She glanced up to see one of the maharajah's friends standing nearby, a small smile on his lips, his dark eyes kind as he gave her a little bow. "Indeed. I am Miss Fine."

"I am Mr. Patel, cousin of the maharajah. My uncle knew the duke and duchess well during their time in India. In fact, he was once of great assistance to them when they wished to make an—acquisition." He tilted his head as he gazed down at her. "I don't suppose that might be of much interest to your project?"

An acquisition, was it? She glanced across the room at Benedict, who watched her quizzically. She gave him a little nod. "I am sure it would be. Their Graces' time in India must be of interest to my readers." She slid over to make room for him to sit beside her on the satin settee. "Indeed, I would like to make India a centerpiece of my article, a great pinnacle in a ducal career, but so far I have not found a great deal of information about it all. An acquisition, you say?"

"Yes. Jewels. Extraordinary jewels, which made a most fascinating journey. The late duke wished most fervently to buy them."

Flora leaned close and said quietly, "If they were the jewels I am thinking of from the old stories, surely they had left your uncle's hands already."

"The diamonds, I am sure you mean. Yes, so they had. But my grandmother once greatly hoped to retrieve them, after my uncle let them leave his possession. When it became clear that would not be possible, she wished to find a way to claim a portion of their price. I suppose I must say it was she, not my uncle, who really helped in their resale."

"How so, Mr. Patel?"

"I am not entirely sure. She went to a Mrs. Stillworth, the owner of the diamonds at that time, and offered to help negotiate with the duke. I believe the lady had come to some straitened circumstances." He looked at his cousin, who was chatting happily with the duchess. "I do not think it came out the way she had hoped. She would have been most happy to hear of their disappearance so long after, if she had lived that long."

"What does your cousin think of it all? Would he wish for the diamonds to be returned to him?"

"He is happy enough to be rid of them." Mr. Patel took two glasses of champagne from a passing footman and handed Flora one. "The curse, you see. Most amusing."

Flora studied the maharajah, laughing and chatting without a care in his handsome world. Or was it an act, like hers was? "I think I may have heard of this curse, and of course it is exactly the sort of thing my readers would want. But does your cousin believe in this curse? He doesn't seem the type. Neither, I must say, do you."

"Oh, of course we believe in them, Miss Fine. Don't you?" He took a sip of the champagne and gave her a secret smile. "Yet there was one rather strange tale I heard, from my uncle right before he died. I was quite young then."

"A strange tale?"

"I have told few people of this, but perhaps you would like to have it for your notes there. Perhaps you might wish to write more of the diamonds, later. I always thought it would make a fine novel."

Flora glanced down at her notebook, as yet too empty for her taste. "I might indeed. Unless you wish this tale to be—more confidential for a time."

"For a time, maybe. I wouldn't wish it to wound

anyone. Yet one day it should be known, if only for its strangeness." He studied her closely for a long moment. "You do have a trustworthy gaze, Miss Fine. Just as the duke said when he sent me over here."

Benedict had sent him? And told him she *trustworthy*? She fidgeted uncomfortably. "Yes—well. Indeed."

"My uncle was a very old man at this time, and he said there was much shock and sadness when the duke's son died so mysteriously and in such a way, connected to the diamonds all those years later. Some said it was the curse. Then, some friends of my uncle told him they saw the duke's son, in Hyderabad—alive. After his reported death."

Flora was shocked. "Alive? Were they quite sure?"

He tilted his head. "Are you suggesting it was a ghost they saw?"

Once, Flora would have scoffed at such an idea. Now, with her unfortunate acquaintance with the late duke, she wasn't so sure. "I don't know. He was found in Cornwall."

Yet he hadn't been. His bones were found, with the remnants his lordship's clothes. What if it hadn't been Benedict's father at all?

"I do not think a ghost can drink chai," Mr. Patel said. "He was seen at a cafe, looking rather ill. Feverish. And a few days later, a body was found, a body in an English suit with light hair. But he had been in the water so long he could not be identified. My uncle was sure this was the duke's son."

"If he died in India..."

"I could not say for certain, Miss Fine. My uncle seemed haunted by the thought, though. I have wanted to share it for a long time, and tonight was my chance to make sure the new duke knows. He said I should tell you anything I need to, and you will relay it to him."

"I shall, of course, Mr. Patel, with your permission."

He smiled, and stood to give her a bow before he went back to his cousin. Flora couldn't do anything at all for a moment, she was so stunned by the idea that Benedict's father had gotten to India after all.

But if he had, who was it in Cornwall? Could he possibly still be in India, not dead at all, even? Maybe his great romance met him there. Maybe...

She shook her head. It was all so blasted confusing! She should stick to seances in the future.

Benedict came and sat down beside her, handing her a fresh glass of champagne. "You look a bit pale, Flora. I thought you could use this. I didn't mean any harm in sending Mr. Patel to speak to you, he just seemed so intent on telling me something and my grandmother was nearby..."

She gratefully gulped down the bubbly liquid. "No, I'm glad he told me, Benedict. It's just—well, you should fetch one of these glasses for yourself. I have something very strange to tell you..."

Fifteen

"What an astonishing place," Flora said, longing to spin around and around to take it all in. "Like a fairy-tale. I can't believe it's all real—or that we've seen so many places lately. I've traveled more in a fortnight than in all my life!" She hoisted her valise up closer and tried to manage Chou-Chou on her leash, as the dog kept trying to dash ahead. Not that Flora could blame her; she, too, had never seen quite such a place, so wild and free and exhilarating, calling her to plunge ahead and see it all. The sea and sky and tall, waving grass.

"The diamonds must have gone on quite the adventure all those years ago, traveling so much," Benedict agreed. "Can you believe, Flora, that we were just at that French casino party, and now we're here?"

Flora stopped to lean on a low, rough, gray stone wall and stared down at the roiling, frothing waves crashing below. Cornwall was indeed wild and strange and windswept-lonely, and she quite loved it all. On the rocky beach below, she noticed a small boat vanishing into a hidden cave, children searching the stones for seaweed.

"Who shall I be this time?" she said. "A reporter

again? That was fun, and people do seem to love talking to a reporter. Or another cousin?"

Benedict also leaned on the wall, watching the sea and the sky with a thoughtful look on his face. He, too, seemed different here than he had in France, with his hair caught and tossed by the wind, his cravat loosened. More free, maybe, as if the hold of the diamonds grew looser here even as they took a step closer to the stones and their fate.

"Maybe we could be a married couple, taking a walking holiday," he said.

"You think I should be a duchess?" Flora said with a laugh, even as the thought of being Benedict's wife (albeit a temporary one) was much too tempting. "No one would believe it."

"I think I would much prefer to *not* be a duke," he answered with a grin. "To just be a mister. Mr. and Mrs. —Smythe. That should do it. Just a person again, as I was before I had to be a duke."

"Mr. and Mrs. Smythe, on a walking tour, staying above the pub, eating our fish and chips supper! Oh, I do like it," Flora said, and she *did* like it. It sounded more like a beautiful, impossible dream than a French casino ever could. "Before I became Madame Flowerdew, I used to daydream about things like that. Just like my little flat, evenings by the fire with a book and some toasted cheese. A nice, scenic walking tour for excitement. Quiet-like. Peaceful."

A frown flickered over his brow as he looked at her. "Was your life never—quiet before?"

Flora studied the gray-streaked sky, but in her mind she saw flashes of old, dirty streets, dusty stages, shabby rooms. "Not very. But I've managed to make something content since then. You'll do the same, I'm sure, once we find the diamonds and your old grandfather settles down and leaves you alone."

He laughed wryly. "Content being a duke? I'm not

so sure. But it has to be done, though. Hopefully I can at least make it something better, something kinder, than my grandparents did."

And for that, he still needed Miss Petrie, or someone like her, and her money. Thus he needed the diamonds. "Do you think your father ever could have liked being the duke?"

"Probably not. You've heard the tales now. He was a wanderer, an idealist. Wild-hearted."

"And you're not?"

He laughed again, and rubbed his thumb over his chin. "I can't afford to be."

"So what do you think of the specific tale that he was, maybe *is*, still alive? That he was in India? It was very shocking when I heard Mr. Patel relate that."

"Shocking, yes. I'm still reeling from the idea." He hoisted up the valise again and led them onward down the rutted lane. "I know I should give up any faint hope of him suddenly appearing, of being able to know him. One rumor is too small a thing. But we have to try to find the truth here, if we can."

"Yes, the truth." Flora ached for Benedict as she watched him, watched his brave smile. "And find the diamonds so you can court Miss Petrie again?"

He shook his head. "Oh, Flora. No matter what we discover here, I know I can't marry Maud. Not now. I know her heart isn't in it, and neither is mine."

Flora's heart, though, soared a tiny bit at those words. "What will your grandfather say about that?"

"He'll just have to lump it, won't he?" Benedict said with a laugh. "Go back to wherever he's dwelling and be quiet."

Flora thought of that howling, cold wind racing around her room. "If only he would."

"I'm sure I'll find someone else to marry in time. Right now, we have to try and find out what happened to my father."

"So we stay in Peniston village as Mr. and Mrs. Smythe. It's near the cave where the body was found; there must be someone here who would remember that, or at least have heard about what happened. We'll have to ask around, but carefully. I can't imagine people who live here, in this tiny spot, trust very easily."

"That's why I'm leaving it to you."

"To me?"

"Of course you. You, Flora Flowerdew, have a unique way of getting people to talk to you. My uncle, Regina, Mr. Patel, even my grandmother. My grandfather, too, really; it was *you* he chose to visit. They like to confide in you. I can't get them to do that."

"I do find people rather interesting," Flora admitted. "Maybe it comes from my stage days!"

He flashed a smile down at her. "And maybe it's just you."

Flora felt her face turning hot, and she hoped she wasn't turning red as a beet. She hurried on, hiding her face under the brim of her straw hat. "We should get to the inn, then, and start making new friends." She gestured to the distant horizon, where clouds seemed to be gathering over the sea. "It looks like weather is coming in."

"Then we really should be on our way, Mrs. Smythe," Benedict said. He hoisted the bag higher under one arm and offered Flora the other, quite like a proper old couple. "I'm very glad we're in this together."

"So am I," she answered. And oh—she really was.

Flora took a deep sip of her ale, and gave a tired little sigh as she studied the common room of the inn. It had grown louder, more crowded as the evening went on, the rafters of the whitewashed ceiling wreathed in smoke, the smell of ale and cider thick in the air. She felt pleasantly tired after walking all day, looking for any caves that might have been involved in Benedict's father's story, or anyone who remembered those days and might offer crumbs of clues. Her notebook was full of fascinating tidbits of conversation and descriptions of beautiful sea views, but nothing solid yet about diamonds and disappearances.

Benedict was chatting with a couple of local men at the bar, his face animated and bright as he laughed and nodded. She thought he did make a fine non-duke. After just a few days in Cornwall, he looked really different, light and somehow free, despite the seriousness of their errand. He said she encouraged people to talk to her, but so could he. In the last days, they had made so many new friends, cottagers and farmers and fishermen, the local squire, milkmaids and vicars, and it was mostly due to Benedict and his smile.

She wondered if he understood his father now, understood his urge to leave his real life behind and keep traveling, keep moving, be someone else. Even if Benedict had too much of a sense of duty to do that same, maybe it helped him know his father a little better. Helped him move ahead with what he had to do.

Just as she should do. She glanced down at her notes, going over the events of the day. She would never make a reporter like Evie, she feared, for they were quite muddled.

Benedict clapped one of the man on the shoulder, nodding solemnly at whatever he was saying. They walked toward her through the crowded room, and Flora put aside her notebook with a smile.

"Flora, my dear, Mr. Rowe here has been telling me the most extraordinary tale," Benedict said, gesturing for his new friend to have a seat and waving for another round of drinks. "He said his father once met Dickon Talbot or someone very likely to be him."

"Did he indeed?" Flora said, leaning forward in interest. Mr. Rowe certainly looked old enough to remember the story of Benedict's father's disappearance and all that happened around it, with his weather-beaten face and wild, waving mop of gray hair. But his gray eyes were sharp and bright as he nodded at her.

"In fact—he has something to show us. Something his father gave him." He gave Mr. Rowe an encouraging smile, and the man silently held up his gnarled hand. On his smallest finger gleamed a slightly tarnished ring, set with a large ruby set in filigree.

It was surely the same ring Richard Talbot wore in his photograph, the one Mr. Talbot the butler said had come from an "admirer," and which he wore on his sixth finger.

"Fascinating," she gasped. "Your father gave this to you, Mr. Rowe?"

"Oh, aye, missus," the man said, taking a deep gulp of his newly arrived ale. "'Twas a strange thing, he always said it had summit to do with those bones that were found."

"The bones in the cave?" Flora said. "Do you remember what your father said about the ring?" She asked, making a note.

"You can ask him yourself, missus," Mr. Rowe said. "He drifts in n'out, true, but he can still weave a tale. Better'n me."

Flora could hardly believe a man who looked as ancient as Mr. Rowe could still have a living father, a drifting one or not. She glanced at Benedict, who nodded. "Let's go, then."

❧

The Rowe cottage looked even older than Mr. Rowe himself, tilting and listing, plaster flaking off here and there, ivy twining around the windows and the garden overgrown, but the light in the windows was pale gold and welcoming in the dusty purple twilight. Mr. Rowe led them into a small sitting room, crowded with old furniture and a tangle of dogs on the hearth-rug, where a man sat bundled in shawls by the fire. He *did* look like the Ancient Mariner, Flora thought, bent and gnarled, and he glanced at them from the same gray eyes as his son over his gray beard.

"Aye, and who is this, then?" he croaked. "If I'd known you was bringin' a lady home, my son, I'd have worn my best jacket!"

"They want to know about the bones in the cave, Da," young Mr. Rowe said, straightening the shawls over his father's shoulders and going to build up the fire. "This man says it was his father there."

The old man studied them carefully with his faded eyes. "Aye, is that so? Interesting days those were, interesting indeed. I could have said a thing or two then, but no one wanted to hear it."

Benedict solemnly shook the man's hand. "I would certainly like to hear it, sir. Anything you have to tell me. I'd like to find out what really happened to my father."

"And so you should, aye. Sit down now, I can't be twisting my neck looking up there. Jory, bring us some ale!"

"Thank you very much," Benedict said. He smiled up at Flora as they sat down across from old Mr. Rowe and listened to his tales of the days when the duke's son and a beautiful lady came to their quiet village, all the excitement—and the horror and subsequent silence when it all ended so abruptly.

"I made some drawings," Austol said. "Not so grand, I be no artist, but it all seemed so daft I knew someone would come asking one day. They seemed too important, those people. I'll find 'em for you, if you come back tomorrow." He poured out more the home brew, but Flora shook her head. She had to be able to walk back to the inn, after all, and she had a terrible habit of singing old music hall songs when she's had a wee dram too much. "Jory here can take you to the cave, too, once it's light enough."

"We would certainly appreciate that very much," Benedict said, his eyes wide with eagerness. "What was he like, this man who came to the village all those years ago?"

Austol was silent for a long moment, staring into the fire as if he drifted back over the years. "'Twas a long while between them coming here and those bones being found. We'd about forgotten about it by then."

"Them?" Flora asked.

"Aye, he had a lady with him. Pretty, she was. Tall, with dark hair. They seemed in love, always holdin' hands and the like. They were asking for someone to take them over to France. She was the one who gave the ring, as payment."

"The woman had this ring?" Benedict said, frowning as if he, too, thought of Dickon Talbot.

"Aye. A foreign name, she had, though I can't remember it," Austol mused. "But she didn't seem foreign. A fine London accent, she had, and plain but good clothes. My wife wanted her cloak that bad."

"Nefertiti, by any chance?" said Flora.

"Aye, that was it. Strange name."

"And did they take this passage to France? Does anyone remember where they went?" Benedict asked, and Flora thought perhaps another voyage to France was in the near future. If they had used France as a jumping-off point to India and maybe beyond.

Austol frowned as if trying to remember. "Nay, that was strange, too. They left, saying they would be back the next month to take passage, but they never come back. Then them bones were found..."

"Were there perhaps two skeletons?" Flora asked. "The man *and* the woman?"

"Not as you could tell, nay. Not as you could see,

the tides had taken some of the bones out, but there was some of the man's clothes. And that ring. If the lady was offering it, she must'ove got it from him." Austol rubbed wearily at his dried-apple-lined face, his eyes growing faded and misty with time. "Right pretty she was, though. Someone thought they saw her a little later, walkin' a lane with a different man, but it must'ove been someone else. Someone..."

"I think my father is tired," Jory whispered. "Come back tomorrow, aye? I'll find those drawings for you, and take you to the cave."

∼

Flora sat with Benedict in the small sitting room between their chambers at the inn, warming her toes by the crackling fire as the wind howled against the old windows. The night outside was wild, the sharp wind and a cold rain brought in from the sea as night closed around them, but inside all was cozy and peaceful, quiet except for Benedict turning the pages of his father's journal and Chou-Chou snoring on her cushion.

It was—nice. Very nice. Too nice. Flora was afraid she could get used to such domesticity. It might be hard to go back to the clamor of London, the real work of ghosts and bill-paying. Of being alone in the evenings. She'd liked being alone for so long, but now, here in this quiet...

Quiet. Startled by the realization, she glanced around all the shadowed corners and into the rough-hewn ceiling beams of the little room. No ghosts at all. In fact, she hadn't seen the old duke in quite a while. It was just Benedict and her.

"Do you think your grandfather has gone?" she asked.

"Hm?" Benedict glanced up, his sky-blue eyes unfocused for a moment with distraction. Then he smiled lazily. "Is he not here? Has Chou-Chou told you something?"

"No, that's just it. I haven't seen him in days and days, not since we left London. And CC seems lazy enough, she doesn't hear him, either."

"Maybe he sees we have matters in hand here—sort of. So he can stay in the ether."

"Letting other people handle matters doesn't seem like him, at least from what I've seen of him. He likes to be in control, doesn't he?"

"Well, he certainly did in life. No wonder my father so infuriated him." Benedict held up the journal. "I feel as if I can come to know my father a bit, after all these years. He always followed his own star, his own ideas."

"And do you think his star ended here in Cornwall?" Flora asked. "In the caves?"

Benedict glanced out the window at the stormy evening, his eyes narrowed. "I don't know. I saw this, on almost the last page before the journal ends." He handed Flora the battered old book.

She put aside her own notebook, where she had been trying in vain to jot down her scattered thoughts, and studied the journal. It was a little pencil sketch, quick and rough, of a lady's face in profile with the cliffs and crashing ocean in the background.

Benedict's father was clearly not an artist, but he wasn't unskilled, and there was a force of deep emotion in every sweeping line. Dramatic and elegant. There was something rather familiar about her, something about the brow maybe, or the longish nose. But it was hard to really tell in profile, and with all the years between the sketch and the present moment.

Nefertiti was scrawled at the bottom of the page. *"The Beautiful One Has Come."* The same as the line earlier in the journals.

"Do you recognize her?" Flora said.

"No. It's definitely not my mother."

"If your father was able to get this journal to Mr. Talbot, after being here in Cornwall, maybe it wasn't him in the cave. Maybe it was this other man someone saw her with, walking in the lanes."

"I would truly like to think he escaped somewhere," Benedict said quietly. "But I'm also afraid to hope even a little. I sent off a message to India before we left France, making some inquiries, maybe we will hear some news soon. I knew my mother and I were never a large part of his life, but would he really vanish forever without a word to me in all these years? Where would he go? And did he—did he..."

"Did he kill someone to take his place in the cave," Flora whispered. "Or maybe Nefertiti did?"

"Or it's her in the cave. They never said it was a man, just that it wore my father's clothes." They sat silently for a long time, listening to the howl of the wind, Chou-Chou's snores, their own thoughts. "What do you write there, Flora?" he said finally.

She glanced down at her notebook. "Oh—not much, really. I was trying to organize everything we know so far, or think we might know. I'm not having much luck, I'm afraid. My mind feels so scattered. Yet I feel as if there's just one little fragment to tie it all together, floating just past my grasp."

"I feel the same way. There is something there, something I'm sure is quite obvious, though I'm too blind to quite see it. Maybe if we wrote down everyone we've met, and the part they might play in all of this..."

"Oh, yes, good idea." Flora took up her pencil again, and wrote: *Suspect One: The Petries*

"All of them?" Benedict said.

"Yes, as of right now. Sir Henry seems to be anxious to see Maud married to you, of course, and Maud doesn't seem so certain. Maybe he is trying to persuade her? Make her see this as some sort of dramatic romance? Or perhaps she is trying to ease out of it."

"Ease out of it?" Benedict said, but he was laughing as he clasped his hand over his heart as if wounded. "I am quite the catch, I will have you know, Miss Flowerdew!"

"Oh, yes," Flora murmured. She did know that, all too well. "And Maud does think you are very nice, just as she is. She wouldn't want to hurt anyone."

"What about Lady Petrie? Why would she want to pretend to be a ghost?"

Flora tapped her pencil on the table, thinking of fluttery, teary Lady Petrie. "I have no idea, unless she thinks she will also push her daughter forward—or end things."

"How would they set up the hoax? It does seem rather well-done."

"Too well-done. I couldn't have set it up so well. Sir Henry seems smart enough, he could have studied up on mediums, I suppose. Still, you are right. If this is the doing of one of them, they are in the wrong profession." She made some notes next to the Petrie name, and jotted down the next. "Lord Edward, and Lawrence and Regina. What if they really *did* want the ducal title? And Regina once lived in India. She might have heard something about the diamonds."

"They seem so welcoming, though."

"Yes, at least Lord Edward certainly is. Regina is very sweet, but she is also quite bored. Ghosts might liven things up for her." But then there was the same question —how did they set it all up? And as far as she knew, they hadn't been in her séance room.

"There's Mabel," Benedict said. "She's in the circus business, she would know all about such things. And she certainly has a legitimate quarrel against my grandfather."

"True. Anger does seem to smolder away there." Flora wrote down the actress's name. "She is rather elderly now, of course, though I'm sure she could hire any number of people to help her. If she thought it would get her the diamond she was promised..."

"And there's Richard Talbot," said Benedict. He shook his head sadly, as if he thought about his old butler. "He obviously had his finger in several nefarious pies, along with his ruby ring. What if he's out there somewhere, lurking, waiting for his chance to find the diamonds? Or what if whoever killed poor old Talbot has taken on Dick's schemes?"

"Very possible indeed," Flora said. "We need to try and find out what happened to Dick. And then there's the maharajah and his friends. He might want the diamonds back, as well. It could very well be part of their purpose in seeking out your grandmother." She jotted down the names of the people they'd met at the casino. "What about your grandmother herself? We never did find out where she gets her money for that gorgeous villa."

"It does amuse me to think of Grandmama fluttering around, pretending to be her husband's ghost," Benedict said, with a deep laugh that made her laugh, too. "It would be a long way to come from France, but like Mabel I'm sure she could hire people. And I know she'd like the diamonds back."

"And that leads us to the mysterious Stillworths, who sold the diamonds in the first place," Flora said. "I wish we knew more about them. But I suppose it's been such a long time, just one impoverished colonial family out of hundreds would be lost. I could write to Mr. Patel, he seemed forthcoming enough, and see if he can find out more about them."

"You see, Flora?" Benedict said happily. "You are the most friend-gathering person I have ever known."

She laughed. "You just talk to them about their favorite topic—themselves."

"I shall remember that. Is there anyone else on our list?"

"I think we have to include most of the people here in Cornwall. If there were diamonds here, they would have heard about it, and lots of people would have wanted them. There might have been a fight, a cover-up of some sort." She sighed. "It does sound rather overwhelming. But at least we know more than we did when we started."

"And we'll know even more soon enough." The little clock on the mantel chimed the hour, and Flora was startled to see how late it had grown. The time flew past while they were cozy together by the firelight.

She carefully tucked the list away in her folder, and stood to stretch. "CC and I should be in bed now."

"Yes, there's lots to do tomorrow." Benedict stood up with her, and to her surprise, her shock of tingling delight, he bent down to kiss her cheek. His lips were warm, soft, lingering on her skin, and she had to curl her fingers into tight fists to keep from grabbing him and kissing him back. "I'm so glad we're on this journey together, Flora."

She stared up into his face, shadowed in the firelight. "I am, too," she whispered. "Very glad indeed."

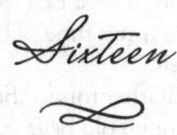

Sixteen

It was a gray, windy, damp-spitting day as they made their way down a steep, cliff-side set of rickety steps toward the caves, but the threatening rain hadn't moved back in yet. Flora moved carefully, holding onto her hat with one hand and Benedict's arm with the other. She was glad she wore her most sensible clothes, a brown tweed suit and flat boots she'd never had a use for before, but she suddenly missed the perils of London. Pickpockets and con artists were nothing compared to Cornwall weather. She was also glad they left Chou-Chou back at the inn, even though she could be useful if there were any ghosts lurking in the caves. Flora couldn't bear it if the little scamp fell into the waves far below and got swept away.

Part of her more cautious self wished she was back there with the dog, too. She wasn't sure she really *ought* to be following these strangers along cliffs to distant beaches. Not that she could really see a choice, not if they wanted to find those caves and move a bit closer to any answers. She held tight to Benedict, and kept following Jory and a couple of his cousins down the steps. The rocky beach looked perilous as well as beautiful, cold wind howling around them.

"Do the tides reach this far?" Benedict asked.

"Only when there's a storm," Jory answered, taking a clutch of torches out of his knapsack. "It's how them bones were found, a bad rain wiped away the boulders they were hid behind. These caves were used by smugglers, you see, before'n my time. They've been deserted since then, pretty well."

"And your grandfather found them?" Benedict said.

"Aye. He was a tough old beggar, but it still gave him a right little shock." He took a clutch of papers from under the torches in his bag and handed them to Benedict. "Here's them drawings, too. Da thought they might help."

Before they ducked into the darkness of the looming caves, Benedict studied the sheaf of yellowing, curling papers in the grayish light. Flora peeked over his shoulder. They were rough, all right, stick-like figures, not detailed, but she could see the lines of bones laid out between tumbled rocks. Some were missing, and the skull seemed caved in one side. A possible source of death, or was that done by the tides? There was also a drawing of the skeleton's clothes, a man's suit, once fine but in tatters, a hat, the ring.

Benedict went very still. "Look," he said, pointing out a small detail to Flora.

She gasped. The bony hand had an extra finger—just like the photograph of Richard Talbot. "I suppose that would explain how the ring came here, if he got it from your father or Nefertiti. Did she and/or your father kill him to throw him off their trail? And then used the body to throw everyone *else* off, too?"

Benedict stared at the cave entrance, his expression cold and blank, as if he looked into an eternity of his own there. "So it wasn't my father there. But what's worse, Flora? A dead father, or one who would bash a man over the head and leave him in a cave?"

Flora gently touched his arm. "We don't know that's

what happened. We don't really know anything at all yet, do we?"

Thunder cracked over their heads, making her jump, and a cold rain touched her cheek.

"Come on, then, Mr. Smythe!" Jory called from the entrance.

Flora tugged at Benedict's hand. "Come on, we should take a look after we've come so far. Or at least stay out of the rain for bit."

He shook his head hard, as if shaking off that past, and nodded. They ran after Jory and his cousins into the musty, salt-smelling cave just as the storm pounded down. It was a low-ceilinged, eerie place, suffused with a greenish light from the torches and the fading daylight, the pebbled floor piled with decayed old crates and the jagged shapes of boulders. She shivered to look at it, to imagine ending one's days there.

"It feels haunted, doesn't it?" she whispered. "We don't need CC here to tell us that."

"Indeed," Benedict agreed grimly. "A dismal place for a tomb."

Flora gently laid a gloved hand on the damp, stone wall, and wished she had the gift of sensing events, emotions. Surely whatever dramatic things had occurred here should leave an imprint. Yet she felt nothing. Just cold.

"This was near the place," Jory said, gesturing to tumble of boulders.

"And the body was just wedged here, between the stones?" Benedict asked as he carefully examined the mossy spot.

"Aye. My granda used to say it looked like he was just coshed on the skull and dragged there, maybe already dead, maybe drowned later, who could say."

Flora shuddered to think of it. What a dreadful scene it must have been, the loud rush of violence, then silence and chill. She hoped the poor man, whoever it was, was already dead.

"Does it seem like a woman could have done it alone?" Benedict said.

"Maybe she lured him here and then surprised him, hit him on the head," said Flora, trying to imagine this was indeed one of her penny-dreadfuls, just a scene in a book, not something that actually happened. "Then she could have been alone, if she was strong enough. Nefertiti looked tall. She glanced back at Jory. "Does anyone remember anything else about the woman, besides she might have been walking in the lane with a man?"

He frowned in thought. "I'm not rightly sure, Mrs. Smythe."

One of his cousins, heretofore silent, said, "Old Benny at the mill once said he rowed her out to a ship in the middle of the night, but he was a bit barmy there in the end, and no one else saw her again."

"Was she with anyone on this boat with Old Benny?" Flora said.

The men glanced at each other. "I don't rightly think anyone ever said."

"But does anyone recall what she looked like?"

"Tall. Dramatic-like," Jory said. "Not pretty so much, but dark hair. A fine nose."

The cousin added, "The kinda woman you remember, I'd say. But I never saw her."

"The nose was big," the other cousin added.

"Not big," Jory argued. "Maybe with a bump, though?"

Flora considered this. "It does sound like the sketch in the journal, and the Egyptian photograph. Was she here with your father? And where on earth did she go?"

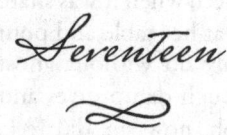

Seventeen

F lora stared out her bedroom window at the
    street below, all gray and foggy and hazy. Rain
    fell, strong and thick like Cornwall, almost
blinding—but this was London rain. She knew she
should be glad to be home, back in her usual habitat, yet
she rather missed the wild sea winds battering outside
while she sat by the cozy fire with Benedict.

She pulled the curtains closed and turned back to
the chamber. Papers and books, the journals she had
borrowed from Benedict, were scattered across a table
she had brought up from the sitting room, and Chou-
Chou was resting on her plump pillows on the bed. The
Pom calmly groomed her paw, as if all her traveling ad-
venturess had never happened at all.

Flora couldn't quite put it all behind her, though.
Once, when she had still been struggling and cold,
dancing her feet off and putting up with greasy men's
leers all the time, her own time and her own space, a job
that didn't involve her backside being pinched, a warm
fire and plenty of good food and wine had been all she
wanted. And she'd gained that, all by herself, and she
was grateful for it every day. She wouldn't want it to ever
change.

Yet somehow, traveling with Benedict, seeing new

places, having a partner to work with, make some mischief with—it had been awfully nice. Better than nice. Fun. Fascinating. It had reminded her how great trouble could sometimes feel, when it was shared.

She sat down at her table and poured out some tea. She could certainly do without ghosts bothering her, and crawling through damp caves and such, but being with Benedict—oh, now she did feel foolish! All after these years of guarding her heart so carefully. And now this! She liked a *duke*, of all people.

A duke that had to marry a suitable, well-dowered lady. Even he parted from Maud Petrie, as he rightly said he must, he would do his duty and find someone else. His sense of obligation would insist on it, and his concern for his people was one of the things she admired the most about him. He was a *good* man, and she had seldom met one of those before.

Flora glanced over at Chou-Chou, who slowly blinked at her as if in understanding. "It's a bloomin' mess, Chou-Chou. I'm afraid it's all my fault." Flora smiled ruefully. "We did have fun, though, didn't we?"

She would have that, forever . France and Cornwall and the circus, fine memories. And hopefully soon the old duke would be back where he belonged, for good and always.

If she could just fit it all together. Something nagged at the edge of her mind, hidden in some strange mist. If she could just grasp onto it...

She took another sip of her tea, and on impulse added a dollop of brandy to it. She glanced over the papers arrayed in front of her, rearranging them in hopes of seeing them differently.

She had the Egyptian photographs, the sketch in the journals, and she examined them under her quizzing glass. She peered at every tiny detail, every blurry bit she could glimpse through the lady's gauzy veil, every pencil line. Every word he wrote about his Nefertiti.

And then she saw it. "No!" she gasped aloud, and sat back in her chair. How had she not seen it before? "Fool, fool! You're such a silly, Florrie Gubbins."

"Have you found the diamonds yet?" a soft voice asked.

Her heart racing, Flora leaped out of her chair, a pen knife clutched in her fist in a most ineffectual weapon. She glimpsed a man's face in the dressing table mirror, hazy as if seen though clouds, but clearly a face, portly, reddened, surrounded by bushy muttonchop whiskers. Like the portrait in the duchess's villa.

He wasn't shouting now, not belligerent, not whizzing around tearing up the room. Even CC just looked at him in quiet curiosity. He seemed, well, resigned. Sad.

"No," Flora said. She didn't let go of the pen knife. She still couldn't trust him. "I have a feeling they've gone forever. But your grandson can surely still safely marry without them. Just not with Maud Petrie."

The duke shook his head. "That milquetoast girl. Probably better off without her after all."

Flora didn't think Maud was such a milquetoast as all that. She was insisting on following her heart, despite her parents' pressure on her. "There are plenty of ladies who would want to be a duchess, with or without the diamonds." And plenty who would marry a handsome bloke like Benedict. "Did you really think there was a curse on the jewels? Your wife seems to be doing fine without them."

The duke gave a most un-ethereal snort. "Of course she is. She'll always land on her well-shod feet. I never had any fear for her. Not like..." His words trailed off, yet he sounded—could it be *wistful*?

"Not like your son."

"He was always a strange lad. I always hoped he would end up well enough."

Flora glanced down at the journals, and a thought

struck her. Yet another thing she should have realized before.

"Have you seen your son, then? Where you are now," she said. "Maybe at one of your card games."

He was silent for a long moment, the clouds in the mirror growing thicker until she wondered if he had left. "No."

"But you've looked?"

"I don't have time for such nonsense! This is a large place, you know. I just wanted my diamonds."

"I'm sure it's quite large. All those centuries crowded around. Yet the diamonds might not be your main concern, I think." She picked up one of the battered journals and waved it around. "You can't fool me now, Your Grace. I'm sure you've learned a thing or two since your life here."

He snorted again. "You are a most impertinent young woman. But yes—I thought perhaps if I could find the diamonds, I could bring my son to me. I never did understand that strange boy in life. No sense of duty, of pride in his family name. His marriage—well, maybe it was a mistake to match him with Isabel."

"And it would be a mistake to match Benedict with Maud."

"If you say so," he said, sounding most disgruntled. Flora had the feeling *I made a mistake* would never pass his lips, dead or alive. "But have you done anything useful at all, except for gallivanting all over France and Cornwall like that?"

"It wasn't all gallivanting. Paris and Cornwall were quite beautiful." She ran the tip of her finger over the sketch of Nefertiti. "But yes, I do think we found something useful."

"Well, then? What is it?"

"You can just come back to a séance tomorrow evening and find out. I haven't quite worked it all through."

"Hmph. If you insist. Whist is getting rather boring." There was a deep, heavy quiet for a long moment. "But, you do think my son is dead?"

"I think he probably is," she said gently. "Just not in the way everyone thought. You should look for him, when this is all over."

"Maybe." That quiet descended again. "And tell Benedict—well, there's a vault at Coutts. Separate from the Everton funds at the Bank of England. It has something he should have, something he needs to make sure Mabel gets. It was—well, very wrong of me not to be sure she received it before."

Flora was speechless. The old duke, being nice at last? It was easily the most astonishing thing about this whole astonishing things about this whole business.

There was a bright golden flash of light, CC growled, and the ghost was obviously gone. Flora shook her head, and reached for her box of notepaper. She had to write to Benedict asking him to help her set up one more séance. It was time to settle this all, once and for all.

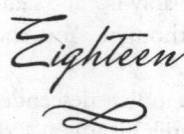

Eighteen

"What do you think, Mary? It's all properly mysterious, I hope," Flora said, propping her hands on her hips as she examined her séance room.

"Oh, yes, miss. Right spooky," Mary answered.

The chamber was draped in purple and black, muffling any light that might appear, the round table draped in more purple and lit with a glass tray of candles that reflected and flickered in the glass. The air smelled of incense, smoke drifting in the faint light.

Flora glanced over at Benedict, who sat on a purple velvet settee with Chou-Chou beside him. "Now, if only my grandfather will make an appearance after you've set the stage so beautifully."

"I think he will. He did seem to really want to make amends when I spoke to him last night," Flora said.

Benedict laughed. "My grandfather? Making amends? I can't wait to see that."

"He wants to make sure of what happened to your father as much as we do." Flora straightened a candelabra on the table, and glanced in the mirror to make sure she, too, looked the part, her black, jet-beaded Madame gown straight and her wig perfectly curled and covered by a lace veil. She counted the chairs, enough for the Petries, Maud, Evie, Mabel, and Chou-Chou. A constable waited patiently behind a screen in the darkened corner.

Then she sat down to wait. She didn't have long before the knock at the door. Mary hurried to answer, and returned to announce, "Miss Evie is here."

Evie rushed in, brandishing a thick folder of documents. "You were quite right, Flora!"

Flora sucked in a deep breath. The last act of this particular Follies was about to begin.

~

"How long must we stay here, anyway?" Sir Henry grumbled as he plopped down in his designated chair. His wife sat on one side of him, subdued and quiet in gray satin, while Maud was on the other, her chin raised defiantly. Miss Priscilla Petrie sat on her brother's other side, glancing around with interest, a half-smile on her lips. Mabel was by Evie, the cherries and silk flowers on her battered straw hat vivid in the shadows. "Just to hear some ghost insult my daughter again over some diamonds? It's absurd. Maudie will be a fine duchess, and I can buy her as many diamonds as she likes..."

"No, Papa, I've already told you," Maud said, quietly but much more firmly than Flora had ever heard from the girl. "I will not be a duchess."

Lady Petrie burst into tears, burying her face in a lacy handkerchief. "Oh, Maudie! If you would only listen..." Miss Petrie handed her a vial of smelling salts.

Maud and Benedict exchanged a long look over the candlelit table. "We spoke this morning," Benedict said. "And we agreed there should be no betrothal between us. I am sorry, Sir Henry."

Sir Henry grabbed his daughter's gloved wrist. "You stupid, stupid girl! What have you done?"

Benedict reached out and gently removed Maud's

175

hand from her father's tight grip. "I know I shall marry one day. But I also know very well I am not the right husband for Miss Petrie."

"I love Charles," Maud insisted. "And I am going to marry him."

"Charles! Charles who?" her father shouted. His face was quite scarlet, and Flora wondered if he needed the smelling salts.

"The vicar, you dolt," Priscilla said, sounding rather bored. "You are always trying to ruin women's lives, aren't you, Henry? Men and all their ridiculous bluster."

"Truer words were never spoken," Evie said.

"I shall be very brief," Flora said, trying desperately to interrupt their family squabble. They had other business to finish. "Though I'm afraid this has little to do with diamonds, really. It has to do with murder."

Everyone stared at her in astonishment, quiet at last.

"Murder of who?" Sir Henry demanded.

"Of my father, in that cave in Cornwall," Benedict said. "Or rather, not my father."

"Though the duke's son *did* die," Flora said gently. "But not in Cornwall. In India. It was the Talbot brothers."

"The Talbot brothers?" Lady Petrie sniffled.

"My family's old butler," Benedict said.

"And his rogue of a brother," Evie added.

"Yes," Flora said. "It was Richard Talbot, you see, who died in Cornwall." She took the photograph from the folder Evie brought, the six-fingered man in the ruby ring. "He was trying to double-cross someone, as was his habit in life, but this time he was the one who was fooled. And his brother simply knew too much, after all these years, despite his quiet, respectable life." She glanced at Benedict, longing to reach for his hand, to comfort him, when she saw the flash of sadness in his blue eyes.

"Then who killed them?" Lady Petrie said. "*All* of them? It's all so strange!"

"It *was* a great puzzle to me, I admit," Flora said. "So many little, shattered pieces, but they never seemed to slot together." She looked around the table, all the confused faces. "It could have been any of you, of course, or several others who aren't here at all. Lord Edward, for example, and his son and daughter-in-law. Maybe they wanted the dukedom for themselves? And Regina was once in India, where all this seems to have begun. The dowager duchess lives beyond her financial means. The duke cheated Mabel from her promised inheritance. The maharajah wanted the diamonds back. And you, Sir Henry, want your daughter to be a duchess above all."

"So *I* am a duchess?" Lady Petrie said, sounding rather excited to be considered so.

"You could have been the grandmother of a duke one day."

"Don't be ridiculous!" Sir Henry blustered. "My wife and I would never give up all we have just for a title, no matter how much it would have been useful."

"So tell us, Miss Flowerdew," Miss Petrie said with a little laugh. "Which of us is a nefarious penny dreadful villain?"

Flora smiled gently. "Like I said, I did feel a fool, until Evie kindly visited the Somerset House record office for me. It was something Lady Petrie once said."

"Me?" Lady Petrie cried. "But you said I am not a murderer!"

"No, indeed. But you told me you once attended Miss Johnson's School for Clergyman's Daughters. That you had lots of proper friends there. Including a girl sent from India when her parents died, I think?"

Lady Petrie dropped her handkerchief and half-rose from her chair, her eyes wide. "I—well, yes."

"What was her name?" Flora said. She took one of the papers from Evie's folder. "Miss Stillworth, was it?"

"No, I think..." Lady Petrie gasped.

"But she didn't stay Stillworth for long, did she? Not when the Petries adopted her. Is that when you met your husband, as well? How young you all must have been. Weren't you—Miss Petrie?"

Everyone turned to stare at Priscilla Petrie, as Mary subtly moved to block the door.

Miss Petrie smiled coolly. "Oh, you are clever putting that all together, Miss Flowerdew." She glanced calmly around, as if sitting in the audience of an operetta. But the little pearl-handled pistol she drew from her tapestry handbag was all too real. "But I can also be clever when I need to. I've had to be, after all that happened in my life. I'm quite sure *you* understand what it is to be young and alone in the world."

Flora took a deep breath, trying to calm the touch of panic deep inside of her. "It was your mother who sold the diamonds to the duke, wasn't it?"

"They were *our* diamonds," Miss Petrie cried, the first hint of emotion appearing in her voice. "Ours. My mother loved them, and she was devastated to let them go. And then we were not even paid what they were worth! It killed her. I saw her, you know, at that séance of yours. So very sad. And I was sent to that horrid school..."

"It wasn't so very bad as that, Pris," Lady Petrie sobbed.

Priscilla glanced at her pityingly. "You were the only one who was kind to me there. Such a gray, cold place. And then the Petries came along and adopted me. A new start, I thought..."

"Ungrateful wench," Sir Henry growled.

"Oh, shut up, Henry, for once in your life," Priscilla snapped. Chou-Chou ducked in the table. "You and your family, you only wanted an unpaid servant, a useful spinster to do your dirty work, take care of your spoiled children. But I confounded you all. I fell in love. *Real* love." Her eyes suddenly sparkled, as if with unshed tears, and she shook her head sadly. "It was a true mingling of souls when I met him. Too high for you mundane sorts."

"But—who was it?" Lady Petrie stammered. "I don't remember any suitors!"

"The duke's son, of course," Priscilla said. "My Johnny. When I took my meager savings and went traveling."

"But then you killed him?" Mabel cried. "That sweet young man?"

Flora didn't take her eyes off Priscilla, or the gun. "He disappointed you in the end, didn't he? Like everyone else."

"We were going to run away to India," Priscilla said. "We had already been to Egypt, you see, when my family thought I was recuperating from the 'flu at Weymouth. It was like a paradise. We could get away from England, you see, from our awful relatives, his sickly wife. But we had no money of our own."

"And that was where Dick Talbot came in?" Benedict said.

"He said he could help us steal and sell the diamonds. Johnny gave him the ruby ring as a down payment. I should have known better, of course—once a con man, always a con man. Once we got to Cornwall, we found out he was going to keep the diamonds and kill us."

"But you killed him first," Flora said.

Priscilla laughed. "Of course! I had a chance for happiness finally. I would never let someone like that ruin it all. Plus it could be made to look as if it was Johnny. No one would try to find us, then, we went off to India. And you could be the duke, Benedict."

"My father..." Benedict began, his voice rough with suppressed tears. "Then he is truly dead?"

Priscilla tossed him a look that was almost pitying.

"I am afraid so. Yet I did not kill him! He disappointed me in the end, it's true. He became convinced by some ridiculous tarot card reader that the jewels were cursed. He wanted to return them to the maharajah's family. Can you imagine anything so silly? He wouldn't listen to reason. Then he died of a fever, and I had to make my way back to England alone." She looked down at the table, her brow furrowed. "I suppose they *were* cursed, in the end."

"And the diamonds?" Sir Henry demanded.

"I don't know. They were gone when Johnny died. Vanished just like my love." She swung the gun toward Sir Henry. "And I had to live with a tyrant of a brother and a spoiled niece! I thought all could be made right when Maud became a duchess, as I should have been. And then that old butler Talbot found out what had happened all those years ago. Some silly old journal. He came to me, demanding the truth. I have no idea how he knew I was Nefertiti. So he had to go, of course."

The gun swung again toward Benedict and Flora. Maud screamed. "It's too late now. Because of you. No one should be the duke if my Johnny is gone. No one!" Priscilla shouted.

There was a great explosion, more screams and shouts, and everything happened in such a swift blur Flora couldn't tell what was going on at all. Benedict grabbed her hard around the waist and knocked her to the floor as the table toppled, candles falling to the carpet and guttering out. Something unseen flew through the air and hit Priscilla on the head. She shouted in rage, and was drowned out by the shriek of a wind whipping around the room, tossing the draperies hither and yon. For an instant, a man stood above her, broad-shouldered, gray mutton-chopped, clad in a paisley dressing gown.

"You shall not harm my grandson!" he shouted. He knocked Priscilla down as she tried to rise.

"Grandfather?" Benedict gasped.

"You bastard!" Mabel shouted. "You promised me!"

"I'm sorry, Mabel sweetums," the man said. "You'll be all right now. We all will." Chou-Chou rushed out from under the table, barking like mad. "Except for you, you mangy little cur!"

As fast as the storm and fury arose, it vanished. The old duke was gone. Flora sat up slowly, holding tightly to Benedict, and saw Evie scooping up the dropped gun and holding it to Priscilla, who was sobbing and kicking at the carpet. The constable who was hiding behind the screen in the corner rushed out to haul her to her feet.

For an instant, everything was perfectly still and silent, the air thick with shock. Then a card fluttered down from the ceiling, the painted lovers entwined. Flora kissed Benedict, holding onto him so tightly she was sure he could never get away from her.

"And I tell you, my girl," Sir Henry shouted. "You will *not* marry any vicar!"

Epilogue

I t was truly a gloriously beautiful wedding. The sun-washed church was filled with white satin streamers and creamy lilies and roses, sending the sweet scent of summer and new beginnings into the air. Maud was radiant as she glided up the aisle on her father's arm, a cloud of tulle and silk. Her mother wept. Charles the handsome young vicar glowed when he took his bride's gloved hand in his at last. The organ swelled with the strains of "The Voice That Breathed E'er Eden."

A perfect day all around. And not a ghostly presence or a single murder to mar it all.

Even Flora, hardened as she always thought to romance, sniffled a bit behind the dotted net veil of her pink hat. Benedict, sitting beside her, slid her a handkerchief.

"Thank you," she whispered, and daintily blew her nose. "Are you not a bit wistful?"

"Wistful?" he said with a puzzled little smile. "Of course not. I rather enjoy weddings. There's almost always cake and champagne afterwards."

"But that could have been you at the altar! Pledging eternal love."

Benedict thoughtfully studied the couple clasping

hands, their starry eyes only for each other. "No, Flora, it could never have been me. Look at them. They are very clearly meant for each other."

And so they were. Maud and Charles were the very image of a romantic novel couple, both so young and gorgeous and glowing with sheer happiness. Flora had always held a rather jaundiced view of marriage. She'd seen enough husbands hanging about the Follies back-stage door *without* their wives. Yet now, watching that blissful couple pledge their troth—she felt a bit sad, happy, glowing warm and wistful all at once.

She glanced up at Benedict, his golden hair like a halo in the sunlight from the stained-glass windows, smiling as he watched the wedding. "Yes," she said. "I suppose things worked out just as they were meant to..."

❧

And, far, far away, in the dark-green, steamy depths of a timeless jungle, in a carved stone temple deep with shad-ows, an ancient statue of Vishnu watched the ever-shifting world with an unchanging eye of a large, sparkling diamond.

Also by Amanda McCabe

About the Author

Amanda McCabe wrote her first romance at the age of sixteen--a vast historical epic starring all her friends as the characters, written secretly during algebra class (and her parents wondered why math was not her strongest subject...)

She's never since used algebra, but her books (set in a variety of time periods--Regency, Victorian, Tudor, Renaissance, and 1920s) have been nominated for many awards, including the RITA Award, the Romantic Times BOOKReviews Reviewers' Choice Award, the Booksellers Best, the National Readers Choice Award, and the Holt Medallion. She lives in New Mexico with her lovely husband, along with far too many books and a spoiled rescue dog.

When not writing or reading, she loves yoga, collecting cheesy travel souvenirs, and watching the Food Network--even though she doesn't cook. She also writes as Laurel McKee. historical Elizabethan mysteries as Amanda Carmack., and Eliza Casey...

Please visit her at http://ammandamccabe.com